Seven At The Sevens

A Collection of Seven-Word Stories, Memoirs and Poems

Written by WritersAnonymous™

Edited by Grant Trenton Gardner

FIRST PAPERBACK EDITION PUBLISHED 2011

Cover Illustration and Cover Layout by Grant Trenton Gardner
Cover Copy by Charles Chestnut and Grant Trenton Gardner
Book Layout Designed by Grant Trenton Gardner and Scottie F. Gerald
Edited by Grant Trenton Gardner
Editorial Assistance by Otis Anderson, Charles Chestnut, Scottie F. Gerald, Temple Goodwin, and M. Zd
Senior Executive Administrative Assistant: Scottie F. Gerald

Library of Congress Cataloging-in-Publication Data

Gardner, Grant Trenton
Seven At The Sevens/by WritersAnonymous™
ISBN: 978-0615492711

WritersAnonymous™

Where dedicated and anonymous writers are heard.

DEDICATION

This book is dedicated to all writers, past and present, anonymous and otherwise, who held the faith and conviction that they had a story to tell and toiled away long before they ever knew what they were writing would materialize into a finished work. With great sincerity, Thank You to all the writers who came before us, leaving pieces of themselves behind on leaves of paper for the rest of us to benefit from and appreciate. This book is also dedicated to the next generation (and after) willing to put thought to paper and like the writers before them, willing to toil away without knowing what will happen.

CONTENTS

Warning: Creativity

ACKNOWLEDGMENTS

We, the writers of WritersAnonymous have decided to stay anonymous. But this does not mean that we cannot be gracious and bring to the forefront every person and organization responsible for the making of this book. We owe our sincerest gratitude to all of the individuals and organizations listed below who chose to believe in our dream and support us long before there was a book to speak of. Thanks to the generous and timely backing from these amazing supporters, *Seven At The Sevens* is now a bit more than wishful thinking. As published authors now, we are finally able to revel in our anonymity.

WritersAnonymous extends its deepest appreciation to all fifteen writers (Lime Andersen, Otis Anderson, Uncommon Bostonian, Charles Chestnut, J. Lindall Derne, Falcon Canthearthe Falconer, Grant Trenton Gardner, Scottie F. Gerald, Temple Goodwin, E. E. Gowings, Pinckney Phillips, L. S. Russell, Myrtie West, Adair Willow, and M. Zd) for submitting highly creative works for this book project. WritersAnonymous also acknowledges the time, effort, and enthusiasm invested by all writers during various stages of book preparation including the fundraiser and book launch.

Further, we owe much gratitude to The Sevens pub, where it all began. For the two years that it took to put together this book (from an obscure concept to a physical publication), The Sevens was our "poetics of space," (to quote the title of Gaston Bachelard's thought-provoking book) providing us with both the much-needed familiarity of place, beer, and food every Tuesday night, and the continued inspiration for creative forays into the vast unknown. So much of *Seven At The Sevens* was conceived and penned because of The Sevens and the times we spent there. We share our special thanks with The Sevens establishment, their wonderful and attentive and humorous staff, Julianne, Ms. lovely Lilly and the barmen, Bobby, John and James for allowing us to make the pub our home away from home and our weekly writers' space. We also wish to acknowledge the anonymous writer at Simon's Coffee Shop for leaving a profound quotation on the bathroom wall. Dear Anonymous Author: whoever you are and wherever you are, know that we thank you for leading us to another marvelous literary destination, *The Poetics of Space* by Gaston Bachelard. We also wish to acknowledge the many hours spent assembling the book at the Parker House, the Boston Athenaeum, in a booth at Bakey's Restaurant downtown, in and around Northeastern's campus, especially the Student Center and Espresso Royale on Gainsborough Street, and two Starbucks in Harvard Square. In addition, we would like to pay tribute to a few places in New York for their inspiration and for keeping us warm and snug inside while it was beautifully snowing outside: McSorley's Old Ale House in the East Village, Vbar just south of Washington Square Park, Pete's Tavern on Irving Place, Fred's at 83rd and Amsterdam Ave, and Nussbaum and Wu in Morningside Heights. And, we'd also like to thank Ken Burns for his inspiration and for the masterful way in which he brings to life a city through the words of Walt Whitman and F. Scott Fitzgerald in his film *New York: A Documentary* with his vivid blend of imagery, music, and narration of poems and other written works.

We would like to take the opportunity to thank with sincere gratitude all of the following authors, writers, artists, and thinkers listed below for leaving pieces of themselves on blank leaves of paper. Even though many of them are no longer with us in person, their timeless contributions and words are still here to influence generations to come: Louisa May Alcott, Muhammad Ali, Woody Allen, Gaston Bachelard, Neal Cassady, Anton Chekhov, Francis Ford Coppola, Rebecca Lee Crumpler, E. E. Cummings, Corinne Demas, Charles Dickens, Emily Dickinson, Frederick Douglass, Bob Dylan, Ralph Waldo Emerson, F. Scott Fitzgerald, Robert Frost, Etienne Gilson, Allen Ginsberg, Nathaniel Hawthorne, Ernest Hemingway, Oliver Wendell Holmes, Sr., Washington Irving, Henry

James, James Joyce, John F. Kennedy, Jack Kerouac, Vivien Kooper, John Lennon, Abraham Lincoln, Henry Wadsworth Longfellow, Robert Lowell, Katherine Mansfield, John Phillips Marquand, Gabriel García Márquez, Herman Melville, Joseph Mitchell, John Nash, O. Henry, Flann O'Brien, Frank O'Hara, Michael Ondaatje, Steven Pinker, Sylvia Plath, Edgar Allan Poe, L. M. Priday, Charlie Rose, Philip Roth, Alan Seeger, George Bernard Shaw, Adam Smith, Gertrude Stein, Nick Stenzel, John R. Stilgoe, Dylan Thomas, Henry David Thoreau, Sojourner Truth, Harriet Tubman, Mark Twain, John Updike, J. H. Van den Berg, Phillis Wheatley, Walt Whitman, Frank Lloyd Wright, and William Butler Yeats.

The completeness and depth of our book relies heavily on the creative talents of two very gifted illustrators who generously dedicated their time and contributed remarkable artwork for the final book. We extend our sincere thanks to Darren Buchanan for his impressive illustration (p.105) and to Kathleen Whipple for bringing several of the seven-word short stories and memoirs to life with her wonderful imagination and poignant illustrations in the Seven-Words section.

We extend a debt of gratitude to Gregory Petsko for his immense faith in our book, and for taking the time to write a thoughtful and enthusiastic foreword that places our book in a literary context in a manner that only he could. We also owe a special thanks to Vivien Kooper and Steven Pinker for their enthusiastic endorsements even during early stages of book preparation. Vivien Kooper (former wife of musician Al Kooper) is a professional writer, author, song lyricist and developmental editor in Los Angeles, CA for more than twenty years. She grew up around the film industry in Hollywood, CA since her father was a special effects professional in Hollywood for more than three decades. Steven Pinker is Professor of Psychology at Harvard University. He has been named Humanist of the Year and Time magazine's "The 100 Most Influential People and Thinkers in the World Today."

To push the book beyond mere idea or dream, we held a fundraiser that sent us on another delightful path of inspiration and discovery. "Ask and ye shall receive" was the message and to our great surprise, both people and local businesses in Cambridge and Boston couldn't have been more supportive. Generous donations and support poured in from every corner of the community—from friends to family to colleagues to other individuals, and from local bookstores to cafés to independent movie theaters to writers' organizations. We offer our sincere thanks to the establishment and staff of Beacon Hill Pub and Scholars American Bistro and Cocktail Lounge for providing us with the venue for our book's fundraiser and book launch, respectively. And, thank you to our enthusiastic friends and family (Joel Gagne, Taylor Teresi, and many many others) who have assisted in spreading the word about our book throughout the east coast (Boston, New York, DC and Philadelphia), west coast (Seattle, San Francisco, and Los Angeles), and elsewhere.

We are tremendously indebted to the following guests (and anyone we inadvertently omitted) for their generous support at the fundraiser: Veronica Alas, Janet Alesevich, Kerstin Barr, Dan Carpenter, Jenny Chung, Kristine Cummings, Leigh Cummings, Tricia Gomes, Katherine Goodwin, Josh Howard, Kim Isbell, Navtej Khangura, Waiming Kuo, Julia Klutkowski, Jeanne Limroth, Ken Maclaurin, Laura Malloy, Marlena St. Martin, Suzanna Matheny, Jim Matheson, Sven Eric Meier, Grant Morris (The man formerly known as bourgeois, Skippy the Bushman, and The Sultan of Satanic Slurs), Kate Murray, Charles Nuss, Isabelle Nuss, Jessica Ormsby, Ellie Peacey, Cris Perez, Jessica Resnick, Henry Ryan, Kirsten Ryan, Arjun Sharma, Ben Sheldon, Anne Shields, Michael Shtalman, Kim Stasny, Seiyam Suth, Katya Tsikhan, Nathan Viles, Susanna Walter, Richard Yieh, and Elena Zalyalpin.

We also appreciate kind donations from the following individuals who were unable to attend the fundraiser: Martin Borbone, Toby Cavanaugh, Sunita D'Souza, Hope Jansen, Nikki Hill, Oliver Holmes (no relation to Oliver Wendell Holmes), Shulin Ju, Ann Killeen, Morgan Martin, and Randy Walther.

In addition, we owe many thanks to the following organizations and establishments in Cambridge and Boston for their generous sponsorship of gifts and prizes at the fundraiser: Brattle Square Theater, Brookline Booksmith, Coolidge Corner Theatre, Crema Café, Diesel Café, Grub Street, Inc., Peet's Coffee, The Harvard/MIT Coop, Kendall Square Cinema, Pavement Coffeehouse, Porter Square Books, Simon's Coffee Shop and Trident Booksellers & Café.

Brattle Square Theater, Grub Street, Inc., Kathleen Whipple, Myrtie West, Charles Chestnut and M. Zd deserve a special mention for their generous gift of silent auction items. Special thanks also to Peter Cook, Jeanne Limroth, Jessica Ormsby, Jessica Resnick,

Kirsten Ryan and Arjun Sharma for their generous purchase of silent auction items at the fundraiser. And, a big thanks to Temple Goodwin for arranging food and refreshments.

A special thanks also to all our guest contributors for their sportsmanship and participation in the seven-word short story and memoir contest at the fundraiser. Hearty congratulations go to our guest authors, Kenton Ethan Clarke, Josh Howard, Grant Morris, Kate Murray, Cris Perez, Richard Yieh, and Ernest Yu whose outstanding seven-word submissions made it into the book!

We also thank Martin Borbone, Mitchell Bragg, Tricia Gomes, and Grub Street Inc. for a constant stream of advice and suggestions during the preparation of this book. And, Rishi Patil, Management Consultant guru, Qun Sui (Sabrina), and Hashim Siraji for their timely help with preparation of promotional materials. And finally, a big thank you to Anne Bost for the generous use of her couch during Hurricane Irene for the book's final final edits.

Lastly, we, the writers of WritersAnonymous are indebted to our parents, siblings, spouses, partners, children, other family members, friends, and literary ghosts, especially the Good Gray Ghost for providing the invaluable (and not so invaluable) inspiration and for contributing to a multitude of life experiences that informed the writing of *Seven At The Sevens*. These anonymous but important people in our lives, in many ways, make us the writers we are today.

—WritersAnonymous

FOREWORD

Lucky Seven

"Since brevity is the soul of wit…" *Is it also the crucible of creativity?*

There are exactly seven words in that quotation, which is, of course from the notoriously non-brief Polonius in *Hamlet*. And there are exactly seven words in the *bon mot* that follows, which, I must confess, is mine. There's something magical—mystical, if you prefer—about the number seven. Seven days in a week. Seven deadly sins. Seven is a winner at dice, unless you are trying to make a specific point, in which case seven is a loser. Aristotle cites seven causes for all human actions: chance, nature, compulsions, habit, reason, passion, and desire. Rome had seven hills. And there are seven words that are the key to making any marriage run smoothly: "You know, dear, you may be right."

Hemingway also invoked the number seven in discussing the craft of writing, when he said that "I always try to write on the principle of the iceberg. There is seven-eighths of it under water for every part that shows. Anything you know you can eliminate and it only strengthens your iceberg." (Elsewhere in this book you will find that he practiced what he preached.)

Which is, I think, the principle behind this remarkable and delightful book. In it, a group of writers who have been meeting weekly at The Sevens pub (a charming eating and drinking saloon on Beacon Hill in Boston) present a series of seven-word short stories, as they call them. The stories represent nothing less than an attempt to encapsulate something true and complete in seven words. I had the pleasure of joining this group, by invitation, one evening and it was the most fun I had in a vertical position in quite some time. The atmosphere reminded me of the great literary salons of the past: Madame de Stael's in late 18th century France, at which you could "meet the world," as one attendee noted; Alice Pike Barney's house on Sheridan Circle in Washington, DC, where in the early 20th century you could find James McNeil Whistler discussing art with Theodore Roosevelt, Enrico Caruso and Sarah Bernhardt—just about the time Gertrude Stein's quarters in Paris were entertaining Hemingway, Scott Fitzgerald, and James Joyce; or perhaps the legendary Algonquin Round Table, which met every day for lunch from 1919 to 1929 at the eponymous New York Hotel, and whose members included Dorothy Parker, Robert Benchley, Edna Ferber, George S. Kaufman, and Harpo Marx (whose brother, Groucho, said of the group, "The price of admission is a serpent's tongue and a half-concealed stiletto."). The point I'm trying to make is that, contrary to the popular image of writing as a loner's profession, literary creativity has often flourished in groups, whose members deliberately try to stimulate one another.

How well this particular salon has succeeded you can judge for yourself. My take is that some of these seven-word "stories" really do stand on their own as complete tales—a notable achievement. "You liked Picasso, I liked Van Gogh." "I love and I do not care." "Cell phone died. So did social life." "I'm recyclable. Been used over and over." "She was cold and I was numb."

But others seem to me not so much stories as great openings for stories that have yet to be written. "This must be what purgatory feels like." "It was the perfect afternoon for worrying." "He liked her and he liked me." "Mom stacked the odds in my favor." "There's no place like away from home." "We've such limited time to be heroes." Not that there's anything wrong with great beginnings. They're a characteristic of nearly every memorable piece of literature. "Call me Ishmael." "The past is a foreign country; they do things differently there." "It was the best of times, it was the worst of times." "He was born with a gift of laughter, and a sense that the world was mad." "Sing, goddess, of the wrath of Achilles." (Notice that they're all short and sweet, and that every word tells.)

So read these seven word stories as both an end in themselves and as a spur to your own creativity. If you can get through more than a page without trying to craft some of your own, you have more will power than I do, and my advice would be to lose some of it. "His good health never discouraged his hypochondria." "Free will is vastly overrated, I've found." "Aren't all dogs better than most men?" "Never let your fear make your decisions." "His tragedy was that life was comical." Those are some of mine.

The greatest line ever penned by an American writer has seven words: "All right, then I'll go to hell." It's from *Huckleberry Finn* by Mark Twain, and when you see the context in which those words were spoken, I'll bet you will agree with me. Anyway, here's my advice. Read this, and be entertained and inspired. (That had seven words. Exactly. Of course.)

—Gregory Petsko

Gregory A. Petsko is an American biochemist and member of the National Academy of Sciences. At MIT and Brandeis, he trained a large number of current leaders in structural molecular biology who now also have leadership roles in science. After completing his undergraduate degree at Princeton University, he received a Rhodes Scholarship and obtained his doctorate from Oxford University with Sir David Chilton Phillips. In April 2010, Petsko was elected to the American Philosophical Society. Petsko is co-author with Dagmar Ringe of the popular college textbook *Protein Structure and Function* (2004). He is also the author of a monthly column in *Genome Biology*.

Most people may not know that Greg Petsko has his own literary tale to tell. After graduating from Princeton, Greg had his heart set on studying poetry as a Rhodes Scholar at Oxford but fate had other plans for him. When he was on board the Queen Elizabeth, somewhere in the middle of the Atlantic ocean halfway between the eastern seaboard of the United States and the shores of England, his advisor, Maurice Bowra, a preeminent scholar and classicist died. So instead of focusing on poetry at Oxford, he went on to earn his doctorate degree in molecular biophysics.

Greg's love of poetry and literature as well as science makes him one of the most influential people in science today because of the way he so thoughtfully begins any discussion.

PREFACE

In addition to being a collection of brief short stories, "this book is a journal of experiences, not written in the experiencing moment but rebuilt out of memory. As we age, the mystery of Time more and more dominates the mind. We live less in the present, which no longer has the solidity that it had in youth; less in the future, for the future every day narrows its span. The abiding things lie in the past, and the mind busies itself with what Henry James has called 'the irresistible reconstruction'... An experience, especially in youth, is quickly overlaid by others, and is not at the moment fully comprehended. But it is overlaid, not lost. Time hurries it from us, but also keeps it in store, and it can later be recaptured and amplified by memory, so that at leisure we can interpret its meaning and enjoy its savour."

—John Buchan, *Pilgrim's Way* (1940)

A SHORT HISTORY OF THE SHORT STORY

"Over the years, the short story has strained against its own definition [with writers] actively questioning and testing the definition [which is] what healthy genres do... Whenever you have a literary definition that [sets] limits, it inspires a [certain] kind of creativity." Writing is a contest of the mind, an intellectual pursuit. "Given the limitations of the genre... —what can be accomplished?"

"If the short story [like the seven-word] is attempting to capture the essence of something important... then concision and selection are going to be key. How writers select and compress" and present their subject matter is largely determined by their individual styles.

"Poe and Hawthorne preceded the European short-story master Anton Chekhov... by several decades." Years later, Fitzgerald and Hemingway drew influence from their predecessors and from each other. But the best of writers learned from their peers only to create styles of their own.

"The American short story has proved to be a sturdy and elastic genre, as [important] today as it was 150 years ago." It's been recast and condensed [into seven-word stories in this case] and yet the core attributes that Poe stressed (p.2) still hold true today.

Corinne Demas is a professor of English at Mount Holyoke College and editor of the *Massachusetts Review*. A graduate of Tufts University, she has a Ph.D. in English and Comparative Literature from Columbia University. The above quotations were taken from her collection *Great American Short Stories: From Hawthorne to Hemingway* (2005).

INTRODUCTION

A Literary Journey And History Of Writers Groups Of The Past And Present In Boston And New York

The Grub Street Fall Free Press ran this advertisement in September 2010: *A manuscript was left unclaimed in a Beacon Hill establishment. Proprietor is publishing it to pay for unpaid beer tab. Coming soon: Book by WritersAnonymous.* (Thank you, Washington Irving!)

What is This? A Book by WritersAnonymous?

WritersAnonymous, a writers' group founded in Boston's Beacon Hill in Massachusetts, wants to commend you for picking up this book (to help settle an unpaid bar tab) and taking a chance purely on the creative expression and merits of fifteen dedicated but anonymous writers, all of whom submitted work for this collaborative book project.

Dear friends and supporters of anonymous writers everywhere: as you will soon discover and appreciate, what you hold in your hands, while lighthearted and witty at times, is an extremely creative and diverse compilation of seven-word short stories, memoirs and poems. While the work may be brief and distilled, each story is filled with powerful language and meaning—literary gems of original and 'Whitmanesque' style poetry and wit. These short stories and memoirs share great insights and observations, as well as stories of great joy, sadness, loss, and despair.

It is interesting to note that, Edgar Allan Poe, who was born near where Boston's Boylston and Charles Streets intersect, discussed his preference for shorter works over novels or epics because longer works were too bulky. Poe believed good writing was firmly anchored in originality, unity, and the creation of a total effect. Originality goes without saying. But unity—the rejection of any verbal embellishment without adding intrinsic value to the piece—and the benefit of shorter works to be read in one sitting ensures the "totality of effect" or complete immersion into the story. Thus, each entry in our book of seven-word short stories, memoirs and poems is to be pondered and savored—admired not only for its artistic expression and originality, but also for its brevity and totality of effect.

Moreover, our book is in the very spirit of Walt Whitman anonymously self-publishing his first edition of *Leaves of Grass* (although, embedded deep within the text he refers to himself, "Walt Whitman am I… an American"). The book was wittily named after a pun used by publishers referring to common works and leaves of paper. A rather modest volume of twelve poems written for the masses, Whitman's first attempt inspired our first edition here, *Seven At The Sevens*, which is also a self-publication of measured works. Needless to say, if you lend your support to this collaborative book by purchasing a copy and sharing it with others, you will be supporting a creative group of freedom writers, much like Whitman, early in his career.

The Genesis of WritersAnonymous

Whitman's influence on this book, however, began much earlier. Somewhere in the very pit of my soul, I have often wondered: Is the universe capable of having an inherent wisdom in it and can it teach us things along the way? An unanswerable question for sure. But this mystery was exactly what I experienced every time I saw the likes of jolly old Walt Whitman with his gray hair and beard; he was clad in workmen clothes sitting there in the grass, or walking by in the Boston Common or in parts of Cambridge. No doubt a homeless man bore a striking resemblance to the Good Gray Poet. And, what remained of this mystery was a never-ending 'ponderance.' Does the universe reveal to us things, perhaps books, films, persons, even ghosts (in this case, a beloved dead poet) along the way, as we need them? Are we held in a place, a job or situation until we have learned what we're meant to learn before we can move on? Abraham Lincoln believed so. He believed that the Civil War would not end until every injustice from the inequality of slavery was repaid on the battlefield.[1] Whether any of this holds true or not, it's best to be watchful because you never know what you might see or find along the way. No matter what we think we know at certain times, we don't always have all the answers. At least not when we need them or want them. At least not consciously. But, if it is half as good as what I discovered from the Good Gray Ghost, you will be grateful as well.

I am with you, you men and women... ever so many generations hence; I project myself—also I return—I am with you, and know how it is. Just as you feel... so I felt...
Closer yet I approach you;
What is it, then, between us? What is... hundreds of years between us? Whatever it is, it avails not—distance avails not, and place avails not.
In the day, among... people, sometimes they came upon me, In my walks home late at night, or as I lay in my bed, they came upon me. I too had been struck...
—Walt Whitman, *Leaves of Grass*

And I, too, had been struck, as I lay in my South Boston apartment one sleepless night. Perhaps Mr. Whitman and the universe were conspiring. Or, was my subconscious trying to tell me something? What power, though, could my subconscious really have over me? And, could it know something that I did not? Perhaps something valuable that would lead me down a path—somewhere I really ought to be. (Knowing what I know now, naive questions indeed.)

In the very spirit of Whitman, I would "be[come] curious, [and] not judgmental" and see where it would take me. To seek for an explanation of what I was experiencing (thinking and feeling), I began reading about Whitman and came across his visits to the city of Boston to meet with Ralph Waldo Emerson. And that is when I learned of the Saturday Club,[2] a legendary writers group that met for many years in the mid-nineteenth century at The Parker House in

---

[1] **Abraham Lincoln's** second Presidential Inaugural Address in Washington, DC on March 4, 1865.

[2] Next time you find yourself in Boston, stop by Parker's Bar inside the Parker House Hotel at 60 School Street, Boston, MA. Also, pop by the Last Hurrah, which by the way, was named after a best selling novel (1956) by Edwin O'Connor and later adapted into a film (1958) starring Spencer Tracy.

Boston. In addition to Emerson, the distinguished group of sixteen notable members included leading transcendentalist Henry David Thoreau, novelist Nathaniel Hawthorne, and poet Dr. Oliver Wendell Holmes, Sr.

After uncovering the history of the Saturday Club, I began spending hours in the lobby of the Parker House, writing and admiring the place for its architecture, its many intricate details, and its transient atmosphere with all sorts of patrons passing through, as well as its place in literary history during the Golden Age of American literature. At that time, Boston was literarily 'The Hub of The Solar System,'[3] as first coined by Holmes and later with slight modification, 'The Hub of The Universe.' Over pints of beer, I began vividly imagining what it would have been like being one among the crowd when Emerson dined there with poet and professor Henry Wadsworth Longfellow. As I'd sit there, I swear I would feel ghostly presence just like anyone who works there today would swear that the place is haunted. It was an extremely powerful experience acknowledging that I was now standing where great literary minds once stood. And, perhaps Emerson and Whitman's ghosts return from time to time, among old friends. It is wonderful to think that the Saturday Club still dines at the old Parker House for convivial reunions.

After many visits to the Parker House over several months, the idea for WritersAnonymous was born:[4]

WritersAnonymous – Not your typical writers group. Ever thought of challenging yourself to write something monumental? A screenplay maybe? Or, a novel even? What about a short story that is poetry? Well, here is your chance. Maybe this is exactly what you've been looking for. And, maybe this time, you'll get it done! When? Tuesday Nights. Where? A Beacon Hill Establishment.

And, ever since I posted the above ad on Craigslist.org in 2008 and later on Meetup.com, one by one they came and since then, a

---

[3] This reference first appeared in *The Autocrat of the Breakfast-Table* in 1858 and was later rephrased by The Boston Globe as 'The Hub of The Universe.'

[4] WritersAnonymous was established one week before Brunch&More, another social group started in Boston. Both groups were founded on the same principles and philosophies of generosity, inclusivity, and diversity.

growing number of anonymous writers have been meeting weekly at The Sevens Pub, a classic Boston establishment in the heart of Beacon Hill. Today, we share wonderfully diverse ideas and insights on writing, on the books and writers we admire, and just about anything on life if we so choose.

From the start, our mission was clear. There were no prerequisites for joining this group. We, the writers of WritersAnonymous, were a different kind of fraternity. We didn't care where you went to school or whether you went to school at all. The only things we cared about: did the writers, though anonymous, have the passion and desire to write and express themselves? Moreover, did they have the willingness to find their original voice? Were they somewhat driven and able to set ambitious yet achievable goals? Did the writers take the group and its members seriously and would they go out of their way to support and inspire the people around them?

WritersAnonymous was in search of other dedicated and determined amateur writers who were serious about writing, telling a story, and creating something worthwhile, and who appreciated being part of a supportive community of creative writers. And why did we set out to do this? The writing was on the wall literally. Pubs to finer establishments from Boston to Brookline to Cambridge were covered with literary passages and poetry reminding us that we were indeed in a literary municipality. It seems not even walls could be spared the prevalent and mighty poets' pen. Inside The Squealing Pig in Boston, grout poetry is prominently displayed (yes, you guessed it) in their bathroom's grout. And to my dismay, the bathroom wall in Simon's Coffee Shop in Cambridge led me down a path that I would not have expected. An almost obscure passage to the right of an uncomplicated sketch of Elvis and below *Sunday Morning* lyrics (Velvet Underground) which reads, "The whole machine; continuously living a solution to problems that reflection cannot hope to solve," (J. H. Van den Berg) led me to *The Poetics of Space* by Gaston Bachelard, a French philosopher and physicist. "In *The Poetics of Space*, Bachelard [demonstrates] that space can be poetry... the shelter for imagination itself... a reader's nook... a nest for dreaming."[5] (John R. Stilgoe) It is then no wonder why so many

---

[5] **John R. Stilgoe** of Harvard University attributed these remarks in the Foreword of the 1994 edition of *The Poetics of Space*.

writers long before WritersAnonymous have been seeking out these special places to congregate, to inform and inspire, to dream up new ideas, new worlds and original characters. These kinds of spaces are a lot more common than you may think. Public libraries and college campuses throughout the world have been taking 'the poetics of space' seriously, even if they didn't know it at the time, as they design and redesign their campuses for the purpose of creating these special nests that resonate "deeply, vibrating at the edges of imagination, exploring [and unlocking] the mind."[4] Long before I knew why these 'poetic spaces' were important, I was perpetually drawn to them for some unknown reason. Now I know that the mind craves them and seeks them out. "In the mind, the formal imagination is fond of novelty, picturesqueness, variety and unexpectedness in events, while the material imagination is attracted by elements of permanency in present things."[6] (Etienne Gilson) Thoughtfully designed architecture and spaces send a powerful subconscious message of reverence and permanence. In essence, a message operating just below the threshold of consciousness but strong enough to influence mental processes and potentially capable of unlocking the creative mind. "In an age of so much homogenized space," (John R. Stilgoe) as human beings and no doubt as writers, we take comfort in these unique communal dwellings, in the feeling that they will continue to exist long after we are gone. And in essence, keeping at least in some part our short legacy here in the physical world alive, and perhaps a place that we dream we will return someday and reminisce over memories of a life well lived.

Today, we are fifteen writers strong! We connect writers with similar passions and the same burning desire to tell a story. We inspire one another to find our own voices through the often lonely and difficult creative writing process. We write everything from novels to short stories to screenplays. Above all, we constantly challenge ourselves to keep going and to write something monumental.

The long journey to WritersAnonymous was indeed a crooked line. As crooked as the murky banks of the Charles River as it winds its way eighty miles to Boston. Boston was supposed to be a stopover

---

[6] A colleague of Gaston Bachelard, **Etienne Gilson** included these remarks in the Foreword of the first edition of *The Poetics of Space* (1964).

on my way from Manhattan to Seattle. In hindsight, though, I had essentially come back to fulfill an old woman's dream of going back to South Boston, the place where she was born and raised. And, to take her on that first trip to Paris that she had always wished for. The following year, she passed away. But not until her last remaining wish was fulfilled. I realize now more than ever that WritersAnonymous owes everything to that dear old woman, Severina. If it were not for her, I would surely be in Seattle and WritersAnonymous would not exist today. Sometimes, paths to nowhere do lead to somewhere.

Looking back on those two years in South Boston, I see that Severina, my grandmother made friends everywhere she went. She would pretend to be drunk on Jameson whiskey (even though she did not drink) and have jovial conversations with the picture of an Irish Prime Minister that hung in a booth inside The Farragut House pub in Southie (It was delightful to watch her cracking up in such carefree and child-like laughter.). And at the Parker House, the doormen quickly adopted her as their own. Whether she befriended the Irish shop girls at the convenience store or they befriended her is besides the point. The point is, she made friends easily and quickly, including people on the street and nearly a dozen women at the senior center. It was quite understandable that because of her, I quickly became the most popular man in Southie with women over seventy. To reference Andy Warhol's famous line, it seemed that my fifteen minutes of fame had arrived. Although, this was not what I expected.

In Paris, I never saw anyone receive more affection than her. My biggest regret is that I was not able to take her back to New York and The White Horse Tavern in Manhattan. She had visited the place back in 1936, at the age of twenty-one, almost twenty years before Dylan Thomas, Jack Kerouac, and Allen Ginsberg hung out there. She would refer to that trip to New York and The White Horse often.

Giving up on Seattle, an experience I was looking forward to (a unique place, and in my mind, a writers safe haven where the overcast gray skies add to its allure and romance, and where the coffee shops resemble old pubs and pubs resemble old coffee shops) was incredibly difficult. But I did it. And, it was this sense of obligation in seeing another person's dreams satisfied that kept me here in Boston. I was satisfied that Severina had a choice. She chose well and so that is what we did.

In the end, it seems that "whether I am on the winning or the losing side is not the point with me. It is being on the side where my sympathies lie that matters. Success in life means doing that thing then which nothing else conceivable seems more noble or satisfactory... And then being ready to see it through to the end."[7] (Alan Seeger)

The Saturday Club and Other Writers' Groups

It is worth pointing out that many writers who succeeded in finding their own voices also formed similar support groups throughout history. In Boston, as I have already pointed out, Emerson, Longfellow, Hawthorne, and Charles Dickens, an occasional guest, along with many others formed the legendary Saturday Club at The Parker House. In Paris, Ernest Hemingway bounced ideas off of F. Scott Fitzgerald and Gertrude Stein. In New York, Kerouac, Ginsberg, and Neal Cassady drew literary influence from one another. Hanging out with fellow writers at the Cedar Tavern in the East Village in 1959, Frank O'Hara recalled, "We often wrote poems while listening to the painters argue."[8]

The New York Influence

Years before Walt Whitman started appearing rather conspicuously in Boston, "in the great city of New York I was walking amid the hurrying throng, and gazing upon the dazzling wonders of Broadway. The dreams of my childhood and the purposes of my manhood were now fulfilled. A free state around me... what a moment was this to me!" Years could be "pressed into a single day. A new World burst upon my agitated vision."[9] (Frederick Douglass)

---

[7] Taken from *Letters and Diary of Alan Seeger* (1917). **Alan Seeger**, perhaps America's greatest unknown poet, was best known for his poem *I Have a Rendezvous with Death*. T. S. Eliot once commented that his college classmate "lived his whole life on this plane [of solemnity], with impeccable poetic dignity..."

[8] In Brad Gooch's biography *City Poet* (1994), **Frank O'Hara** went on to further describe the Cedar Tavern: "There is nowhere in the world now where such a place could exist, tolerant and cheap enough for artists to gather..."

[9] Appeared in *My Bondage and My Freedom* (1855) by **Frederick Douglass**.

nested in nests of water-bays...
an island sixteen miles long
The down-town streets, and... the river-streets
A million people—manners free... open voices—hospitality...
...The beautiful city, the city of hurried and sparkling waters!
The city nested in bays! my city!
(Walt Whitman)

I was extremely fortunate to find myself hanging out with dedicated writers while living in Manhattan. These writers, graduates of New York University, Northeastern, and Columbia, had set out to write their first novel, play or collection of short stories. In many ways it was college for adults. There was never a dull moment with such a diverse community and constant stream of smart, fun, creative types always surrounding us. To take breaks from our literary pursuits, we would invite all of our friends and have a big picnic in Central or Riverside Park. We would socialize and play wiffleball or touch football all afternoon. Often we would spend Saturdays walking from Columbia (116th and Broadway) all the way downtown. We would meander, zigzagging—taking in the side-streets and the avenues as we made our way downtown, serendipitously discovering all kinds of cool places and personalities along the way. Sometimes we would grab coffee or a drink and something to eat and then continue on our way. We even held a relaxed monthly book club of sorts on Saturday afternoons at some low-key café or pub like The West End Tavern near Columbia or the Cedar Tavern in the East Village, places that Kerouac, Ginsberg, and Bob Dylan frequented. If we were not discussing writers, books or films, we were discussing what we saw on Charlie Rose the night before, actualizing that potential gift inherent in every thoughtful conversation we heard on his show. Even more so when the conversations felt free and limitless, and when the views were different than our own, but given ample time to be seriously considered, these conversations challenged us to think differently and to expand our beliefs. To many of us, Charlie Rose and our long walks were as much a part of the fabric of New York as Central Park or the Empire State Building.

Late nights, "when the streets [became] rhythmical perspectives of glowing dotted lines... hanging there against the black sky"[10]

---

[10] Taken from *When Democracy Builds* (1945).

(Frank Lloyd Wright), we'd head to the Underground Lounge in Morningside Heights, where West End Avenue meets Broadway. At the time, the Underground was still mostly a coffee house that held diverse open-mic nights. We'd go listen to L. M. Priday, a wonderful undiscovered local poet at the time whose work reminded us of Frank O'Hara and Emily Dickinson.[11] I'd sit there, holding on to every one of her tactile words as she read them aloud. We called her 'L' and long after the readings were over, we'd hang around discussing poetry with her for hours. One of those late nights, when most everyone else had gone home, it was so peaceful it was surreal. As if it were right out of Edward Hopper's *Nighthawks* (1942). With a glass of red wine in her hand, I remember her saying softly, "Stillness dwells in the darkness before dawn." I remember it as if it were only yesterday. She "had a lively, sharply sculptured face, brown eyes that were alive and wavy brown hair that was brushed back from her fine forehead and cut thick below her ears and at the line of the collar of the brown jacket she wore. She was kind, cheerful and interested, and loved to make jokes..."[12] (Ernest Hemingway) She was the most gifted natural poet I ever heard. I still "...carry [her and] the place... in my heart but sometimes I try to shake it off in my dreams."[13] (F. Scott Fitzgerald)

Sometimes, we would head to McSorley's Old Ale House (est. 1854). I don't think there's another place in New York that has been written about more: a place where Presidents Abraham Lincoln and John F. Kennedy, and Beatle, John Lennon stopped by for a drink.

---

[11] Although **Emily Dickinson** was a prolific poet, she was very private. Fewer than twelve of her nearly eighteen hundred poems were published during her lifetime.

[12] In *A Moveable Feast* (1964), a memoir published posthumously, **Hemingway** writes about life in Paris during the 1920s among fellow writers, Gertrude Stein, F. Scott Fitzgerald, and James Joyce.

[13] *Tender Is the Night* (1934). The title was taken from the poem *Ode to a Nightingale* by the English poet, John Keats. It was **Fitzgerald's** final novel and was first published in Scribner's magazine. A second version was published posthumously according to notes that Fitzgerald left behind (1951). The first version of the novel used flashbacks while the second version was written in chronological order.

In his 1923 poem, "I was sitting in mcsorley's," poet E. E. Cummings famously described:

I was sitting in mcsorley's. outside it was New York and beautifully snowing.

...the slobbering walls filthily...

...Darkness it was so near to me, i ask of shadow won't you have a drink?

(the eternal perpetual question...

...i was sitting in mcsorley's It, did not answer.

Outside. (it was New York and beautifully, snowing...

Years later, I returned to The Old Ale House with members of WritersAnonymous, and one time, armed with a copy of Joseph Mitchell's book *McSorley's Wonderful Saloon* (1943) when "outside it was New York and beautifully snowing" sixteen inches during whiteout conditions. We sat there huddled warm and snug inside while we read aloud Mitchell's prose to see what was still there and if it looked the same. Amazingly, it had not changed.

Sometimes we'd head over to Pete's Tavern on Irving Place and sit in the very booth where the master of short stories, O. Henry wrote "Gift of the Magi." We'd sit there over burgers and pints discussing our writing and reading the framed newspaper clippings about O. Henry that hung on the cluttered dirty old wall. When the weather was especially nice, we'd grab our books to go read on the steps of the Columbia library, at the Central Park Boathouse or under a tree on Cedar Hill. At times, we'd continue the evening at our favorite 24-hour diner, talking with Pete, the old man and our friend behind the counter. Pete always remembered our names and what we liked. It was the coolest thing—all of us sitting there, talking with Pete.

The Sevens and Beacon Hill

Today, WritersAnonymous does the same: Tuesday nights seven at The Sevens. Local rumor has it that The Sevens first opened its doors in 1933. But even while it was named The Colonial Café for many indeterminate years, it was affectionately referred to as The Sevens by the locals due to its location at 77 Charles Street in the heart of Beacon Hill—a neighborhood known for its wealth, famous residents, Federal-style rowhouses, red brick, and gas-lit street lanterns. In 1937, John Phillips Marquand's *The Late George Apley*, a Pulitzer Prize-winning novel, offered one of the best satirical and fictional descriptions of the upper-class residents on Beacon Hill. This historic neighborhood is not unfamiliar to great writers and thinkers of all creeds. Only blocks from the pub, Louisa May Alcott, an American novelist best known for *Little Women* lived at 10 Louisburg Square. Poet Robert Frost resided for a time at 88 Mount Vernon Street. Other notables, such as Dr. Oliver Wendell Holmes, Robert Lowell, Sylvia Plath, and Nick Stenzel lived there as well. In his beautiful poem "Nesting," Stenzel captures a moment on The Hill:

> ...the winged shutters tucked neatly into their nooks
> to let in early spring light, I glance up and down
> Chestnut Street at the naked trees whose names
> I mostly do not know, whose unripe buds are yet
> laboring with promises of delicate blossoms...

The north slope of the Hill was home to abolitionists and profound writers, Frederick Douglass, Harriet Tubman, and Sojourner Truth, who would speak at the African Meeting House on Joy Street. Rebecca Lee Crumpler, a resident of Joy Street, was the first African-American woman to become a physician in the United States (1864). And, Phillis Wheatley of Boston was the first published African-American poet (1773).

The old pub sits at the foot of the old Hill where, just on the other side, Charles Street met the salt marshes of the old Massachusetts Bay before it was filled in with dirt from the top of Beacon Hill. Since The Sevens opened, not much has changed except for its name and the occasional additions to its walls and taps. When you walk in the door, you get the impression that this place is from a different era, as if you stepped back into history. There's something special about The Sevens; it's hard to deny it. Call it whatever you like, but it's unmistakable. According to The Sevens' staff, about sixty people and counting have met there and gotten married. What's the mystery? According to John the barman, "this place is an asshole-free zone!" As you may have already guessed, John is the quintessential Boston barman, never at a loss for a witty remark. When John was asked why the pub doesn't serve burgers, he said with a smile, "Because I don't want grease and smoke making a mess of the kitchen. Besides, customer service is fourth on my list." With characters like John, we often find ourselves plenty amused. Speaking of characters, there's also Julianne, our noble waitress. To be sure, Julianne is not just any waitress. She's also a guest contributor to our book (and a graduate of Connecticut College).

Julianne, Ms. lovely Lilly and the barmen, Bobby, John, and James take very good care of us. As soon as we enter the pub, we often find our favorite beers waiting for us at our table because Julianne will have beaten us there.

In college, my friends and I went to The Sevens and many other local establishments such as The Pour House (because we were cash poor), Flann O'Brien's where we could sit among great Irish writers like Joyce, Shaw, and Yeats (their portraits were sketched in great detail in pastels on large sheets of black slate that hung on the pub's dimly lit dark red walls), and the classic hole-in-the-wall Punter's Pub—with an actual hole in the wall used for ordering food from the adjoining pizzeria. A few of us even took to the road. In DC we'd convene at the Tombs, which was situated near the entrance of Georgetown, and at the Brickskeller off of DuPont Circle, not far from the White House. While studying abroad we would gather at the Lamb and Flag, one of the oldest pubs in all of London. The Lamb and Flag was a special place. Despite being formerly a hangout for numerous dead poets and writers, it was hard to find, tucked neatly away down a dark long narrow alley. We'd gather in the farthest booth in the back and dream of bright futures and all the possibilities, including writing. In each and every one of these places we'd waste no time thinking up the next great story or in having one of those philosophical, life-altering conversations—the kind where we were so sure we were onto something, but only to find ourselves back in the same place again the following week. Years later, we found ourselves in Philadelphia frequenting the Ten Stone, just across the bridge from U. Penn at 21st and South Street. And we filled the place with amusing debates and conversations. My pal, Dennis and I eventually left Philly and went *on the road*[14] heading west for Hollywood. Hollywood was fine and all, except for being inundated with sad actors.

---

[14] **Jack Kerouac** turned his own travel experiences into his celebrated work *On the Road* (1957).

Well, I now find myself in the same place again, the place where it all started. Not in a million lifetimes did I think that I'd return here, many years later and under such different circumstances and with a whole new group of friends who seem much more like dear old friends, even a fraternity of sorts. Today the members of WritersAnonymous are my confidants, "the ones who never yawn or say a commonplace thing, but burn, burn, burn… exploding like spiders across the stars"[14] (Jack Kerouac). They are my writerly fraternity. And, Tuesday nights seven at The Sevens feels like coming home.

Whether we are speaking of The Sevens, or the Parker House or any one of the aforementioned destinations, these places are not merely a pub or a grand old hotel. These are spaces to congregate, converse and even toss about different thoughts and ideas. These are the places where great ideas are born, perhaps, the greatest of all. The founders of this great nation would meet at the Green Dragon in Boston and the City Tavern in Philadelphia to discuss the birth of a new nation. "A new nation, conceived in Liberty, and dedicated to the proposition that all men are created equal."[15] (Abraham Lincoln) A nation governed by its people, for the people.

Mathematician and Nobel Laureate, John Nash at first isolated himself from the social aspects of life while at Princeton because he did not want to be distracted by them. But the inspiration for his theory, which later won him the Nobel Prize, did not strike when he was left alone to ponder but rather occurred while he was out with classmates and was grounded in his observations in the real world. This is well depicted in the film *A Beautiful Mind* in the pub scene where Nash modifies Adam Smith's thesis on economics, which he is able to visualize, while his friends are trying to win over the blonde.

These gathering places are far from what they seem on the surface and should not be diminished for what they appear to be—merely eating and drinking establishments. Instead, they offer spaces to connect and to engage. They are poetic spaces, nests to dream. They are also places to share and to test one's ideas, often in passionate yet respectful discussion. And, "The [truest] test of a first-rate intelligence is the ability to hold two opposed ideas in the mind at the

---

[15] In the less-than-300-word *Gettysburg Address* (1863), considered brilliant for its message and brevity, **Abraham Lincoln** left an indelible imprint on the minds of all nations.

same time, and still retain the ability to function."[16] (F. Scott Fitzgerald) Although with that said, it is often easier said than accomplished because it takes practice.

Hemingway and the Six-Word Story

"For sale: baby shoes, never worn."

—Ernest Hemingway

In the 1920s, Hemingway's friends challenged him in a bar to write a story in only six words. They bet him that he couldn't do it. And, they paid up. Who knew so much could be said in so few words? Hemingway, the master of brevity is rumored to have considered his six-word short story his best work.

Hemingway's famous six-words and his belief in beginning every story by writing one true sentence—that which allowed him to go on from there—led to the creation of the Six-Word Memoir project, several publications, and a National Public Radio special in 2008.

The Seven-Word Short Story, Memoir and Poem

Since WritersAnonymous has been meeting at seven at The Sevens for years now, we decided it would be fitting to put our own seven-word twist on the six-word story idea. Fitting everything that you want to convey into seven words isn't as easy as you might think. Try it yourself. Like Hemingway, keep a pad of paper and pen everywhere you go. Over time, you'll learn to embrace the challenge with both trepidation and delight, and will eventually find your groove. Just like Hemingway's pursuit of finding that "one true sentence,"[12] you'll begin seeing and hearing seven-word stories everywhere. And, when you finally nail your first one, you will be amazed, even bewildered and left grasping the weight of the powerful imagery and meaning of the seven-word that you've just written. Your greatest insight will come from the realization and knowledge that you do not need a lot of words to convey something poignant and powerful. This especially holds true when you write from places of sadness and even despair because in such depths lie the rite of passage to places where the greatest truths are revealed. (Good

---

[16] Taken from *Handle With Care*, which appeared in *Esquire* magazine (1936).

writing not only demands originality, keen observation and wit, it demands emotion!) Learning to write when happy or depressed is essential. As hard as it is, learning to express yourself in all moods will reveal your full range and potential as a writer.

However, when dealing with such limited space, you'll learn quickly that "the difference between the almost right word & the right word is really a large matter—it's the difference between the lightning bug and the lightning."[17] (Mark Twain)

The Box Night

The group devised a creative, peer-review ceremony to ensure a quality check on which seven-word stories would end up getting published and, at the same time, allow for fate to play its serendipitous role in choosing the random order in which the seven-word stories would appear in the book.

The 'Box Night' events, of which we had many, were indeed a spectacle! Patrons of The Sevens would often come over and inquire curiously as we conducted our Box Nights over pints of beer and dinner. We'd randomly place about fifty of our anonymous seven-word story submissions, printed individually on strips of paper, in a box or, in many cases, our classic Microsoft tote bag.[18] Each writer would then take turns in drawing a seven-word out of the secret ballot and reading it aloud. Then we'd proceed by casting a quick and unbiased majority *Yes* or *No* vote based on our gut instincts on whether the seven-word story should be included in the book or not. Regardless of the results of the *Yes/No* vote, we'd have a brief discussion on each seven-word and cast a second vote immediately: an A, B, or C grade. The entire peer review process was recorded by pen and paper during the Box Nights and then transferred to an Excel spreadsheet for final score calculations. All seven-words that made it into this book, except each anonymous writer's three Free Passes and numerous Editor's Picks, received a *Yes* vote and had a GPA of 3.0 or better. The three Free Passes offered writers a chance to include in the book a small sample of his/her own creative

---

[17] In *Letter to George Bainton* (1888).

[18] Little did we know that the reusable Microsoft tote bag would become such an integral part of our Box Night festivities as our makeshift box.

expression and original work, regardless of how peers voted. This freedom—freedom of expression—was important to our endeavors, as many writers' works throughout history have often been neglected early on, only to receive praise over time. It is interesting to note that today Walt Whitman's *Leaves of Grass* and Herman Melville's *Moby Dick*, considered by many to be two of the greatest works of American literature, were not well received in the beginning. However, today they are both revered worldwide.

As you read, thinking and considering each of the following seven-words, remember they can be thought of as self-contained entities or, as Hemingway believed, only the beginning of something more. Perhaps, each seven-word could be the beginning of a short story, a novel, or a screenplay, or just be savored as it is. So it is entirely up to you to decide how to ponder each and every one of the seven-words to follow.

We hope that you enjoy the process that led us here, and that you are as inspired by what you find within the following pages as we were by the amazing writers who inspired us. And, when you and your crew of writers, beatniks, "creatives," or whatever-you-choose-to-call-yourselves decide to gather, good luck and Godspeed. And, if you so happen to see the Good Gray Ghost, be sure to tip your hat to him.

The past and present wilt—I have fill'd them, emptied them.
And proceed to fill my next fold of the future.

I concentrate toward them that are nigh, I wait on the door-slab.

Who wishes to walk with me?

I depart as air, I shake my white locks at the runaway sun,
I effuse my flesh in eddies, and drift it in lacy jags.

I bequeath myself to the dirt to grow from the grass I love,
If you want me again look for me under your boot-soles.

You will hardly know who I am or what I mean,
But I shall be good health to you nevertheless,
And filter and fibre your blood.

Failing to fetch me at first keep encouraged,
Missing me one place search another,
I stop somewhere waiting for you.
—Walt Whitman, *Leaves of Grass*

—WritersAnonymous

SEVEN-WORDS

Delusion is believing your star never sets.

—Pinckney Phillips

Dirty boots, whiskey bottle, nightfall: drunk again.

—Otis Anderson

Bi-coastal, semi-bohemian, quasi-dilettante finally commits to passion.

—Charles Chestnut

Always on a deadline and behind schedule.

—Grant Trenton Gardner

Accept failure. I need to keep moving.

—Kent Ethan Clarke

Brick wall, my head doesn't hurt anymore.
—Charles Chestnut

A window left ajar, your calling card.

—Otis Anderson

Death to me: if I don't contribute.

—Grant Trenton Gardner

Being too creative led to strange encounters.

—Uncommon Bostonian

Alone, morose, yet content, until you arrived.

—Pinckney Phillips

As love ends, emptiness slowly creeps in.

—M. Zd

Do not pressure me with uncompromising expectations.

—Grant Trenton Gardner

Music is the stability in these times.

—E. E. Gowings

"Dr. Teeth," carved on the bathroom door.

—Otis Anderson

Can't always be right. Definitions keep changing.

—Lime Andersen

Birth and Death are equally worth celebrating.

—Myrtie West

Being one of the guys has disadvantages.

—Lime Andersen

Aloneness is given; take it from me.

—Charles Chestnut

Always am somewhere between here and there.

—Otis Anderson

Deep within her eyes a story resides.

—Kent Ethan Clarke

Content alone, content with someone, both
desirable.

—L. S. Russell

A life equals 29,999 days counting backwards.
—Grant Trenton Gardner

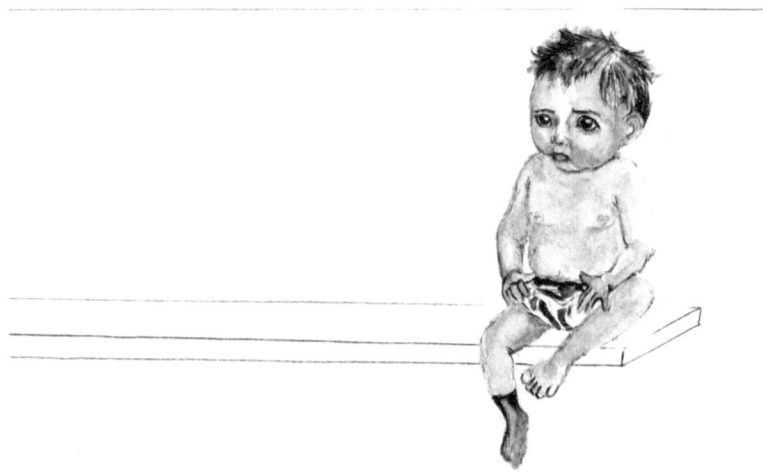

Cramming it all in and perpetually late.

—Temple Goodwin

Customer service was fourth on their list.

—Temple Goodwin

Compassion: I choose to see human frailty.

—Grant Trenton Gardner

An explorer of both world and self.

—Temple Goodwin

An apple a day... still got cancer.

—Lime Andersen

Devotion is my new word for "doing."

—Myrtie West

Courage came later, but not too late.

—Temple Goodwin

Can you have too many houseplants, really?

—Pinckney Phillips

Can I show you, really show you?

—Adair Willow

Amazing how a dog's presence fills space.

—Myrtie West

Could I leave all of this behind?

—Pinckney Phillips

Dating hasn't been very healthy for me.

—Lime Andersen

A piece of the life puzzle lost.

—Adair Willow

Death bed confession: Nana had another husband.

—Temple Goodwin

At 50 years, he can't sleep anymore.

—Uncommon Bostonian

All of this commotion quiets my mind.

—J. Lindall Derne

A sea of headstones beckons to us.

—Kent Ethan Clarke

Betraying and concealing feelings in one breath.

—Scottie F. Gerald

Blond guy won't gray for love, yet.

—Charles Chestnut

Record. Stop. Listen. Recover. Repeat. Get better.

—E. E. Gowings

Being different was the cause of wars.

—Uncommon Bostonian

Don't talk to John, love him, though.

—Otis Anderson

Beautiful like the smiles of atrocity survivors.

—J. Lindall Derne

Being delusional leads to stalking and murder.

—Uncommon Bostonian

Been kissing frogs for years. No prince.

—Lime Andersen

An echo ringing more loudly than life.

—Pinckney Phillips

At age four, learned to miss home.

—Otis Anderson

Bleary eyed, disheveled, must pull myself together.

—Kent Ethan Clarke

Been on red, green, blue, orange, silver. (inspired by the Boston
MBTA)   —Scottie F. Gerald

Always on schedule but still misses deadlines.
                                                     —Adair Willow

Being different is meaningless unless it's authentic.
                                          —Grant Trenton Gardner

Creative writing, feels like holding your breath.
                                          —Kent Ethan Clarke

Another perfect day of doing absolutely nothing.
                                          —Otis Anderson

Cell phone died. So did social life.
                                          —Lime Andersen

I mean things that I don't say.
                                          —Grant Trenton Gardner

I live my life via subway tunnels.

—Lime Andersen

Finally got the hang of self reliance.

—Otis Anderson

I keep waiting for something to click.

—Adair Willow

I leave myself everywhere I ever go.

—Charles Chestnut

He had an incorruptibility that begged corrupting.

—Pinckney Phillips

I am asking that I be saved. (inspired by Jack Kerouac)
—Kent Ethan Clarke

I am complicated and I am easy.

—Grant Trenton Gardner

I long to be understood, not accepted.

—Kent Ethan Clarke

Don't push me to nurture inner failure.

—E. E. Gowings

Haven't got what it takes. Don't care.

—Otis Anderson

How many years till I'm considered wise?

—Lime Andersen

I just wanna be a female superhero.

—Lime Andersen

I know truth when I say it.

—J. Lindall Derne

He liked her and he liked me.

—Scottie F. Gerald

I feel therefore I am still alive. (inspired by Rene Descartes)
—Grant Trenton Gardner

His empty glass remains by the bed.
—Pinckney Phillips

I am definitely not what I seem.
—Grant Trenton Gardner

I imagine worlds without TV and BlackBerries.
—Kent Ethan Clarke

Experience is a matter of someone's perception.
—Uncommon Bostonian

Flowers have power, but booze always woos.
—Charles Chestnut

How it began: one night of boredom…
—Otis Anderson

I am the sum of my imperfections.
—Grant Trenton Gardner

Her mood, fragile as a soap bubble.

—Temple Goodwin

Expect the unexpected! Whom are you kidding?

—Scottie F. Gerald

Fake smiles, just too many to count.

—Scottie F. Gerald

I'm fascinated by both grace and style.

—Kent Ethan Clarke

Every night, we wonder where you are.

—Otis Anderson

Forever wondering, forever wandering, hoping and believing.

—Grant Trenton Gardner

Females on ice are not well accepted. (inspired by the game of hockey)

—Lime Andersen

I defended him, but he never reciprocated.

—Uncommon Bostonian

I am everything... and I am nothing.

—Kent Ethan Clarke

I'm always losing things in my pockets.

—Grant Trenton Gardner

Good words spoken, best words left unsaid.

—Scottie F. Gerald

I am the biggest hypocrite of all.

—Grant Trenton Gardner

Ducking from strong gusts of herd opinion.

—Scottie F. Gerald

He seems just right. I'm wrong again.

—Scottie F. Gerald

Exhale, it could be worse or better.

—L. S. Russell

Dying of loneliness and no one knows.

—Otis Anderson

I admit, I sin every single day.
—Kent Ethan Clarke

Feel like a bohemian though I'm not.

—Grant Trenton Gardner

Feels like I'm hurling toward the sun.

—Kent Ethan Clarke

I couldn't live with having been humiliated.

—J. Lindall Derne

Far more handsome without glasses, but dangerous.

—Otis Anderson

Everyone eventually ends on the discount rack.

—Pinckney Phillips

Freedom is overrated, I'm hungry for dependence.

—M. Zd

Got used to the speed of life.

—Kent Ethan Clarke

Lost in my own thoughts... need directions! (inspired by tripping
down a flight of stairs)   —Grant Trenton Gardner

Genetic zip code, weekends at the Gramercy.
                                                      —Grant Trenton Gardner

Hopelessness is believing your star never rises.
                                                      —Pinckney Phillips

Going against the grain smooths the surface.
                                                      —Lime Andersen

Good books and friends: life's better rewards.
                                                      —Scottie F. Gerald

Friendship with him was a lonely experience.
                                                      —Uncommon Bostonian

Hat revolutions come and go, newsboys remain.
                                                      —Charles Chestnut

I love to get lost in Boston.

—Lime Andersen

Everything we don't do has its consequences.

—Grant Trenton Gardner

Grasping the weight one word can hold.

—Temple Goodwin

Good for you, that's what they say.

—Otis Anderson

I chose to see all her humanity.

—Grant Trenton Gardner

I don't mind a great many things.

—Grant Trenton Gardner

Freedom: relinquishing the ones that got away.

—Charles Chestnut

I love and I do not care.

—M. Zd

Five years ago, my first envelope arrived.

—Otis Anderson

Hope is better for me than religion.

—Lime Andersen

I am freed only by my humility.

—Grant Trenton Gardner

Beneath smog and palm trees, California dreaming.

—E. E. Gowings

I gave up everything to prove nothing.

—J. Lindall Derne

He exists as my interpretation of him.

—Scottie F. Gerald

Forgive my imperfect reconstruction of the event.

—J. Lindall Derne

Every attempt stunted and every dream dashed.

—Pinckney Phillips

Good advice: is there such a thing?

—Scottie F. Gerald

I admire people that I've never met.

—Kent Ethan Clarke

Green buds, blooming roses, turning leaves, snowflakes.

—Charles Chestnut

I am a secret agent of history.

—Charles Chestnut

Enjoy seeing the world from my feet. (inspired by L. M. Priday)

—Kent Ethan Clarke

Getting in touch with my inner dyke.

—Otis Anderson

How are they okay, but not me?

—E. E. Gowings

Gay men and sugar saved my life.

—Pinckney Phillips

I'm happy because I have no choice!

—Scottie F. Gerald

I am held captive by my ego. (inspired by William and Henry James)
—Kent Ethan Clarke

Heart moves a little faster than body.

—Lime Andersen

In the throes of an existential crisis.

—Adair Willow

I'm recyclable. Been used over and over.

—Lime Andersen

Life is about standing out, not falling-in-line.

—Grant Trenton Gardner

Life's extraordinary moments have sometimes gone unnoticed.

—Scottie F. Gerald

If I don't contribute: death to me.

—Grant Trenton Gardner

Listen, my heart beats in a whisper.

—Charles Chestnut

Left on Marion, right on Mixville. Home.

—Otis Anderson

Learned paths are made simply by walking.

—Temple Goodwin

Last call, the finality I didn't want.

—Pinckney Phillips

Inspiration struck, ran and left me broken.

—Pinckney Phillips

Is hope delusional or is that faith?

—Grant Trenton Gardner

I'm tired of the doors being locked.

—Lime Andersen

Let's keep words out. Let's communicate instead!

—Scottie F. Gerald

If I try to act cool, Crash! (inspired when spilling a glass of red wine over a white tablecloth)   —Kent Ethan Clarke

It's over. Time to paint the walls.

—Lime Andersen

It was the perfect afternoon for worrying.
—J. Lindall Derne

I've had enough irony. Give me steelry.

—Lime Andersen

Why exactly did I do that again?

—E. E. Gowings

Writing is one long, slow, hard slog.

—Grant Trenton Gardner

Late nights, pontificating at South Street Diner.

—Grant Trenton Gardner

I've experienced some muted variety of joy.

—J. Lindall Derne

I never believe a word he says.

—Pinckney Phillips

If I became a dictator, be frightened.

—Grant Trenton Gardner

I would have been better off afraid.

—J. Lindall Derne

I'm trying to imagine not feeling sadness.

—J. Lindall Derne

I spin those stories all too well.

—J. Lindall Derne

I swear I'll seize the day soon.

—Adair Willow

I used to know so much more.

—Adair Willow

In my peripheral vision, I see déjà-vu.

—Charles Chestnut

I've come a long way for consolation.

—J. Lindall Derne

I must go but I love staying.

—M. Zd

I played her over and over again.

—Scottie F. Gerald

Left U.S., and let a decade slip.

—Otis Anderson

How exactly do I know you again?

—E. E. Gowings

I wish someone could proofread my life.

—Adair Willow

I ventured a guess, was pleasantly surprised.

—Temple Goodwin

I'm not pretending; I'm really this flawed.

—Grant Trenton Gardner

Ideal outside, flawed inside; how to know?

—L. S. Russell

I still have little tolerance for histrionics.

—J. Lindall Derne

I'm weary of carrying other people's shame.

—J. Lindall Derne

I've woken up too tired to fight.

—J. Lindall Derne

Instruction manual: how to build a soul. (inspired by Annie)
—Grant Trenton Gardner

Don't just hide. Avoid being found out.

—E. E. Gowings

I'll fight for what is not mine.

—M. Zd

I want Dorothy's dreams when I fall.

—Lime Andersen

I want to believe all he says.

—Pinckney Phillips

I'm proud of my cat's name: Clawdia.

—Myrtie West

In dreams, I always fly to Nepal.

—Otis Anderson

I think much more clearly on trains.

—Kent Ethan Clarke

In relationship; intimacy escaped us long ago.

—Otis Anderson

I am trapped within my own perspective.

—Grant Trenton Gardner

I'm running as fast as I can.

—Kent Ethan Clarke

Jumps in heart first, rarely regrets it.

—Temple Goodwin

I'm in a constant state of training.

—Lime Andersen

If I am not involved, I'll perish.

—Grant Trenton Gardner

I wish people would stop underestimating me.

—Lime Andersen

I'll never be yet I must be.

—Grant Trenton Gardner

O Manhattan! My Metropolis! Liberty! Liberty! Liberty!
(inspired by Walt Whitman)   —Grant Trenton Gardner

Only took one to rock my boat.

—Scottie F. Gerald

Making money was an impossible career goal.
                              —Uncommon Bostonian

Outbursts in the shower rarely solved anything.
                              —Pinckney Phillips

O Manhattan! Liberty! Life! Ecstasy! Sleepless nights!
(inspired by Walt Whitman)   —Grant Trenton Gardner

My dog introduced me to good people.

                              —Myrtie West

My pen died. It needs a funeral.

                              —Lime Andersen

New friends that seem like old friends.
                              —Kent Ethan Clarke

My memory is full and not responding.

                              —M. Zd

My lungs require both music and air.

—Adair Willow

Madness and delusions were his best friends.

—Uncommon Bostonian

Making too much of what could be.

—Pinckney Phillips

Raised Catholic, Buddhist now with no tattoos.

—Otis Anderson

Others' perception of me is a curse.

—Kent Ethan Clarke

Mom stacked the odds in my favor.

—Scottie F. Gerald

Mistake's the same. Only names have changed.

—Pinckney Phillips

My father never said he was proud.
                                    —Lime Andersen

Moved on before landlord could collect rent.
—Otis Anderson

Machu Picchu in the rain: electric green.

—Temple Goodwin

Michael could be a talk show host.

—Otis Anderson

Money's running out, but I'm not stopping.

—Otis Anderson

Earthquakes. Tornados. Hurricanes. Floods. Blizzards. Frizzy
hair.   —E. E. Gowings

My storage is unique; I live there.

—M. Zd

My weakness is my only real virtue.

—M. Zd

Perhaps we were star crossed after all.

—Grant Trenton Gardner

My girlfriend is in love with Ricardo. (inspired by the ideal lover, a fictitious polo playing Argentinean)　　—Grant Trenton Gardner

Planting pennies, hoping for a money tree.

—Lime Andersen

Our egotism revealed to us our humanity.

—Grant Trenton Gardner

Pray you don't make the same mistakes.

—Grant Trenton Gardner

My Bluetooth talks to my wi-fi hi-fi.

—Kent Ethan Clarke

My biggest problem is too much faith.

—Grant Trenton Gardner

More experienced? Simply older? Time will tell.

—L. S. Russell

Only glimpses of me are ever revealed.
　　　　　　　　　　—Kent Ethan Clarke

New York City, my eternal love affair!

—Scottie F. Gerald

Liberty: our greatest achievement, not technological superiority.
(inspired by Albert Einstein)   —Grant Trenton Gardner

Oh, to have that talent to waste.

—J. Lindall Derne

Passions, obsessions, perceptions, dreams and sorrows, resistance.
—Grant Trenton Gardner

My parents mostly led by great example.

—Scottie F. Gerald

Meaning well differs from meaning no harm.

—J. Lindall Derne

No one is perfect, not even me.

—Grant Trenton Gardner

Not a morning person, but fake it.

—Otis Anderson

Old pains are living in my chest.

—Adair Willow

My fickle spark seems to be back.

—Adair Willow

Plucking guitar strings in an empty room.

—Charles Chestnut

There's something fundamentally sad about dusty pictures.

—J. Lindall Derne

The despair never overcomes the hopeful hours.

—Pinckney Phillips

There's no place like away from home.

—Pinckney Phillips

My lack of expectations always gets fulfilled.

—M. Zd

From one coast to another, still confused.

—E. E. Gowings

Happiness is a process not a product.

—Charles Chestnut

Ten toes, ten fingers—far from normal.

—Otis Anderson

Nothing is sexier than a big tipper.

—Julianne

Constantly running from yourself is super exercise.

—M. Zd

Perception: it is just another person's reality.

—Grant Trenton Gardner

Reading books is still good for you.

—Lime Andersen

She was cold and I was numb.

—Grant Trenton Gardner

Success, a disease with a weird ending.

—M. Zd

She who constantly wonders where time went.

—Adair Willow

World on his arm, all inked in.

—Temple Goodwin

Romantic purgatory feels like a disconnecting flight.

—Charles Chestnut

The mind: a universe of misunderstood perceptions.

—L. S. Russell

The truth waits in all things always. (inspired by Walt Whitman)

—Kent Ethan Clarke

Sitting in an empty diner at 4:00 a.m.

—Grant Trenton Gardner

The rock song caused his nervous breakdown.

—Uncommon Bostonian

The lingering scent and wanting weren't enough.

—Pinckney Phillips

Someday I'll actually be my Facebook profile.

—Pinckney Phillips

Yesterday: a one word memoir for today.

—Falcon Canthearthe Falconer

What I want for Christmas is un-wrap-able.

—Adair Willow

Tumultuous Boston winds turn umbrellas into sails.

—Pinckney Phillips

Truck bed was filled with traveling bohemians.

—Otis Anderson

Winter, cold, leafless; nothing left to give.

—Grant Trenton Gardner

Welcome to life. Here's your protective equipment.

—Lime Andersen

We were 'positive' we were onto something.

—Kent Ethan Clarke

Trust me, you'll save time being yourself.

—Grant Trenton Gardner

We are infinite flashes of our hopes.

—Grant Trenton Gardner

Vietnam: a country or my way out?

—M. Zd

We are a society of exhausted people.

—Adair Willow

Unplug and interact with people for once.

—Lime Andersen

We walked every inch of that city. (inspired by New York City,
London, and Paris)   —Grant Trenton Gardner

We're all eventually submitted for somebody's approval.

—J. Lindall Derne

When determination dissipates, where does it go?

—Adair Willow

Very little about me is a constant.

—Grant Trenton Gardner

Shoot for real success, not realistic success.

—E. E. Gowings

Why can't they just read my mind?

—E. E. Gowings

This wasn't home, but now it is.

—Otis Anderson

Too caught up in what I am.

—Pinckney Phillips

We are barbarians but with more sophistication.

—M. Zd

We must 'choose' the path of humility.

—Grant Trenton Gardner

Why? I do not know. Do you?

—Kent Ethan Clarke

Wind sings to me less often now.

—Adair Willow

Waiting for life to begin again, again.
—Pinckney Phillips

Vagabonds of wisdom, unite! Will you please?

—M. Zd

Two months, Big Sur, detangled my marriage.

—Myrtie West

Was close to replacing trying with doing.

—Adair Willow

Sometimes I'm this close to life's meaning.

—Adair Willow

She cares. What more can you say?

—Grant Trenton Gardner

Teased, taunted, titillated and left to dry.

—Pinckney Phillips

Short on time and frequently lacking motivation.

—Adair Willow

Seems my toughest critic isn't always me.

—Scottie F. Gerald

The average day can be so strange.

—J. Lindall Derne

Remind me of the things I'm not.

—Pinckney Phillips

Stalemate, I am often held in check. (inspired by Abraham Lincoln)
—Grant Trenton Gardner

Baked beans, cream pie, chowder. My colony.

—E. E. Gowings

Things feel surreal, and then they don't.

—Otis Anderson

Sober up to see your life firsthand.

—M. Zd

Simplicity is my idea of perfect elegance.

—Scottie F. Gerald

The grass is not greener over there.

—Grant Trenton Gardner

Spent New Year's Eve alone and meditating.

—Otis Anderson

The wrong person who seems just right.

—Scottie F. Gerald

Sometimes I don't know what I'm thinking.

—Adair Willow

Sometimes no answer is the best answer.

—Pinckney Phillips

The road less traveled cannot be paved.

—Charles Chestnut

Some exist only within their own wounds.
(inspired by Robert Bly)   —J. Lindall Derne

Sometimes you're the one in the fishbowl.

                                    —Lime Andersen

Thirty-two with no desire to grow up.

                                    —Scottie F. Gerald

When wisdom comes, dreams dissolve for real.

                                            —M. Zd

What do we value but forget soon?

                                            —M. Zd

You liked Picasso; I liked Van Gogh.

                                    —Otis Anderson

Used to party, now let liver rest.

                                    —Otis Anderson

She was a woman of loose transitions.
—Pinckney Phillips

When does overwhelming like become true love?

—Pinckney Phillips

What is love? Absurdity of being human.

—M. Zd

Walking through memories wondering why I've stayed.

—Adair Willow

Those old trees there knew my grandfather.

—Grant Trenton Gardner

Late after work, peace is never realized.

—M. Zd

This is me even though it's not.

—Kent Ethan Clarke

We like to tell ourselves comforting tales.

—Scottie F. Gerald

We've such limited time to be heroes.

—Kent Ethan Clarke

Why do meaningless things mean so much?

—Grant Trenton Gardner

When things crumble, I hit the road.

—Otis Anderson

Tuesday nights at seven at The Sevens.

—Grant Trenton Gardner

EDITOR'S PICKS

Wish I could remove all blind spots.

—Kent Ethan Clarke

Contortionists have easier lives than most people.

—Lime Andersen

Beauty echoes, laughter rings, kindness embraces silence.

—Charles Chestnut

California dreamin' on a Boston winter's day.

—Charles Chestnut

Never lacking justifiable cause for perpetual complaining.

—E. E. Gowings

A lack of creativity was their doom.

—Uncommon Bostonian

A ragtag band of writers telling tales.

—Temple Goodwin

Cooking was a requirement, not an art.

—Uncommon Bostonian

Art instructors stressed proportion. I see disproportion.

—Kent Ethan Clarke

Believe in karma. What goes around eventually...

—Kent Ethan Clarke

Can you see me, really see me?

—Adair Willow

You have more power than you know.

—E. E. Gowings

An abrupt stop to a building crescendo.

—Pinckney Phillips

Buddhist non-attachment is meant for the strong.

—L. S. Russell

Dreams are illusions of things being real.

—M. Zd

Thought Sophia Loren was disguised as Mom. (inspired by Mom)
—Kent Ethan Clarke

Please don't go all "colonial" on me.

—E. E. Gowings

All things changed just when I did.

—Temple Goodwin

Delighting in the highs, weathering the lows.

—Temple Goodwin

Awake! Act! Every moment bursts with possibility.

—Temple Goodwin

A pen dies. Where does it go?

—Grant Trenton Gardner

Confusion brings many questions; I like confusion.

—L. S. Russell

Be grateful, be grateful, be more grateful.

—Grant Trenton Gardner

Creativity spawns when it is least expected.

—L. S. Russell

I have to be fake to succeed.

—Lime Andersen

I am an idealist with(out) any illusions. (inspired by JFK)
—Grant Trenton Gardner

I miss her now that she's gone.
—Grant Trenton Gardner

I fell hard—listening to your stories.
—Otis Anderson

I have a storm in my belly.
—Adair Willow

Fat squirrels. I'm buying a heavier coat.
—Pinckney Phillips

I am simple and I am complex.
—Kent Ethan Clarke

Beneath a velvet salmon splatter of clouds.
—E. E. Gowings

At Seven Eighty-nine West End love blossomed.
—Kent Ethan Clarke

I am in therapy. Who is giggling?
—M. Zd

I love settling into a foreign city.
—Kent Ethan Clarke

Feeling grounded, a tough accomplishment right now.

—L. S. Russell

I exemplify code switching at its finest.

—Lime Andersen

Birth, a construct given. Experiences fill it.

—Grant Trenton Gardner

I believe in God but not religion.

—Lime Andersen

I am a good resource because I care.

—Kent Ethan Clarke

My possessions are portable for frequent moves.

—Lime Andersen

NY or the universe: what's the difference?

—Scottie F. Gerald

Her ears burned at very awkward times.

—Pinckney Phillips

Empathy is for highly evolved, experienced people.

—L. S. Russell

Favorite comfort food: chocolate milk, grilled cheese.

—Temple Goodwin

Handling things on your own was impossible.

—Uncommon Bostonian

Green tea and sandwiches, our last afternoon.

—Otis Anderson

Full of self-absorption, my blog shut down.

—M. Zd

I love silly grins. They're always sincere!

—Scottie F. Gerald

Living at home was an incredible pain.

—Uncommon Bostonian

Laughing at the sculpted goddess is freeing.

—Pinckney Phillips

Is it bad that I can't multi-task?

—Lime Andersen

Let's do it over Grappa, Michael said.

—Temple Goodwin

Initially take responsibility for everything. Later, delegate.

—Myrtie West

Living becomes effortless around people I like.

—Scottie F. Gerald

Life is Thanksgiving and I'm a turkey.

—M. Zd

I'm sweet but I love bitter foods.

—Myrtie West

Wait long enough and death is inevitable.

—Grant Trenton Gardner

Lost look is back in my eyes.

—Adair Willow

Kindness was her greatest quality to witness.

—Kent Ethan Clarke

In Delhi, chasing after monkeys stealing laundry.

—Temple Goodwin

Manhattan in early morning, after the blizzard.

—E. E. Gowings

John Wayne caught my cat's total attention. (inspired when cat was engrossed by a John Wayne movie)

—Uncommon Bostonian

I'm in denial and I admit it.

—M. Zd

I've always lived on the third floor.

—Otis Anderson

I suffer from atmospheric pressure most days.

—Lime Andersen

Wish I could find my "on" switch.

—Adair Willow

I notice things others seem to miss.

—Kent Ethan Clarke

I've pens that have their own story. (inspired by a pen left over from a broken engagement) —Kent Ethan Clarke

Goal is to always love the plateau.

—E. E. Gowings

Two Arlington Street, Cambridge: love surprised us.

—Kent Ethan Clarke

Let's forget it all and never finish.

—M. Zd

Comparisons render competitive misfortunes in life-long friendships.
—E. E. Gowings

I would least like to be close-minded.

—Grant Trenton Gardner

I'm tired of feeling other people's fear.

—J. Lindall Derne

Lyrics… genius and deep or on drugs?

—L. S. Russell

Magic 8 ball: holds no right answers.

—Otis Anderson

My veins should hum, not run silent.

—Adair Willow

Nothing as counterproductive as too much effort.

—Scottie F. Gerald

Perfection is lost; the unattainable is obtained.

—L. S. Russell

My ego always gets in the way.

—Grant Trenton Gardner

Nothing plus nobody equals "the eternal freedom."

—M. Zd

My second favorite Starbucks is a bank. (Broadway & 102nd St.
Inspired by Ernie)   —Kent Ethan Clarke

Life's meaning is found in random places.

—L. S. Russell

Mystified by ins and outs of love.

—Scottie F. Gerald

People with the greatest power often deceive.

—Kent Ethan Clarke

Our personalities are made of infinite vignettes.

—Grant Trenton Gardner

Parenting is not for the anxiety prone.

—J. Lindall Derne

Owning up to who I am daily.

—Kent Ethan Clarke

Many of our social conventions lack logic.

—Adair Willow

Peace and quiet is an expensive luxury.

—Lime Andersen

Makeup is my version of war paint.

—Lime Andersen

Pretending to like wearing shiny sparkly things.

—E. E. Gowings

My biggest problem is letting people in.

—Grant Trenton Gardner

Open wide, insert foot! All too often.

—Kent Ethan Clarke

Seventy Seven Charles Street, Beacon Hill, Massachusetts.

—Grant Trenton Gardner

Mom is texting from the other room.

—Lime Andersen

Rebuilding myself from the pieces left behind.

—Pinckney Phillips

Seductive chuckles always have a final catch.

—Charles Chestnut

She owes her humility to great sorrow.

—Kent Ethan Clarke

Thinking a bit too much these days.

—Temple Goodwin

Just for you, I won't puke here.

—E. E. Gowings

Seemingly wise, can learn more from experience.

—L. S. Russell

Teaching is often more difficult than learning.

—J. Lindall Derne

She always hoped he thought of her.

—Pinckney Phillips

Thin walls lead to too much information.

—Pinckney Phillips

Snapshots of life overheard on the subway.

—Temple Goodwin

The ineluctable modality of the visible—what?

—Charles Chestnut

Scent lingers like a delightful second skin.

—Pinckney Phillips

Not wanting is as painful as longing.

—Kent Ethan Clarke

Trying to put eggs in different baskets.

—Scottie F. Gerald

Who knew me + you = divorce?

—Otis Anderson

To be me or not to be.

—Charles Chestnut

Who is in charge? It's nobody's business.

—M. Zd

Never satisfied, he would always be alone.

—Kent Ethan Clarke

Want to help and be exclusive screwer?

—M. Zd

When did I become the universal scapegoat?

—Adair Willow

This must be what purgatory feels like.

—Lime Andersen

What do I know? I'm afraid little.

—Grant Trenton Gardner

Through the new viewfinder, everything is fresh.

—Pinckney Phillips

You're organized. I am your messy muse.

—Otis Anderson

Westward watching clouds dancing as light fades.

—Pinckney Phillips

Thrives in chaos; less good boxed in.

—Temple Goodwin

We were greater than our individual personas.

—Grant Trenton Gardner

Striving to achieve my potential is exhausting.

—Pinckney Phillips

Searching for the meaning; it's nowhere found.

—M. Zd

Run away every day, but leave notes.

—Charles Chestnut

Self discipline was not her strongest suit.

—Temple Goodwin

They were like playgrounds for adult bullies.

—J. Lindall Derne

Stressed, depressed, judging, overeating, tired: me again.

—M. Zd

The ring of fire is my friend.

—Pinckney Phillips

Seemed like nice people, at the beginning.

—L. S. Russell

Injustices are wrong even behind closed doors.

—Kent Ethan Clarke

My memories: sunny-side up Raspberry Beret on.

—Otis Anderson

Some subjective decisions I'd hate to admit.

—Scottie F. Gerald

Shopping is the second therapy to nothing.

—M. Zd

Sleep apnea unfairly blocked my creative side.

—Uncommon Bostonian

The writing will reveal it to you.

—Myrtie West

See what is... not what I want.

—L. S. Russell

Short whole milk latté, light foam please! (inspired by a four-year search for the perfect cup of coffee)   —Scottie F. Gerald

Running to stand still: day begins again.

—Grant Trenton Gardner

Few seem to have their own style.

—Grant Trenton Gardner

Slurpees heal hurts better than any Band-Aid.

—Lime Andersen

Sandalwood and citrus notes, and Holly Golightly.

—Charles Chestnut

Story of my life, everybody plus me.

—Adair Willow

Often wonders what's seen in my eyes.

—Adair Willow

We like to believe in endless possibilities.

—Scottie F. Gerald

Writing tames the racing mind in self-reflection.

—L. S. Russell

When we lose, we start over again.

—Otis Anderson

What is it like to be carefree?

—Lime Andersen

Thoughts unmasked, unveiled. Speak up, you loony!

—M. Zd

Those who **OVER**— compensate murder my energy.

—Grant Trenton Gardner

I'd obsess if I had more time.

—Kent Ethan Clarke

Striving for excellence, yearning for soulful rewards.

—E. E. Gowings

My heart is smarter than my head.

—Myrtie West

Rain soaked trees, incense and granola. Oregon.

—E. E. Gowings

Layers of neon-blue conversations at The Field.

—Charles Chestnut

Their dislike of her prevented her promotion.

—Uncommon Bostonian

Boston State of Mind: bricks, history, connections.

—Charles Chestnut

Take a breath to expire past frustrations.

—Charles Chestnut

Love is being not guilty of anything.

—Uncommon Bostonian

Whirring, spinning, laughing, rising, collapsing and rest.

—Pinckney Phillips

I never, ever want to stop laughing.

—Adair Willow

A universal dilemma can still feel isolating.

—Myrtie West

Opportunities x Effort / Life = Fate

—Grant Trenton Gardner

Talking amongst ourselves often led to contempt.

—Grant Trenton Gardner

Her insecurities raged, manifested in conceited remarks.

—Kent Ethan Clarke

Heart-broke, being absurdly delusional kept me sane.

—Kent Ethan Clarke

Living through other people. A pen's life.

—A Pen

Sometimes paths to nowhere lead to everywhere. (written at Parker's Bar inside the Parker House)   —Grant Trenton Gardner

So many dream, yet so few succeed. (written inside the Parker House during an impromptu champagne toast)   —Ernest Yu

There was a heartbeat; then there wasn't.

—Richard Yieh

I'm working it out on a napkin.

—Kate Murray

Internally famous but stranger to my family.

—Grant Morris

Jumping aimlessly through hoops for other people.

—Josh Howard

I wish you wished what I wish.

—Cris Perez

ABOUT THE AUTHORS

The Mississippi River inspired Samuel Clemens' childhood dream of becoming a steamboat pilot. It was also the source for the author's pen name.[19] "Mark twain" was what the leadsman on a riverboat called out when the water was two fathoms deep (12 feet), which is deep enough for safe passage. Mark Twain became both Clemens' writing name and a persona that he perfected in his works, particularly in his travel books *Roughing It* and *Innocents Abroad*. In honor of Twain, the writers of WritersAnonymous have decided to take pen names. Fitting that many of our names were taken right out of the Beacon Hill neighborhood, which has served as our place of inspiration and home away from home. It is also fitting that the many hours spent writing this book's Introduction and editing its content and layout were spent inside the Parker House, where Emerson and Longfellow, and the rest of the Saturday Club gathered, and on the fifth floor of the old Boston Athenaeum, one of the nations oldest libraries and a place Nathaniel Hawthorne said was haunted after witnessing what he believed was a ghost.

While it is entirely possible that great and noble literary ghosts assisted the writing of this book, the writers of WritersAnonymous are indeed very real. Who are we? We are multi country—Russian,

---

[19] In *Life on the Mississippi* (1883), Samuel Langhorne Clemens describes how he chose Mark Twain as his pen name. Before settling on Mark Twain, Clemens also went by Josh and Thomas Jefferson Snodgrass.

Indian, Guatemalan and American. We are multi-state—California, Connecticut, Maryland, Massachusetts, Ohio, Washington DC, and Washington State. We are Asperger's and ADD. We are Asian, Latin, black, brown, yellow, and white. We attended Babson, UC Berkeley, Colby, Colorado State, Mount Holyoke, Emerson, Harvard, Lesley, Southern Connecticut State, Washington, Oregon, Suffolk, Regents College London and University of London: Goldsmiths College; PSG College and MS University in India, Princeton, Oxford, Northeastern, UMass Amherst and New England Conservatory. We are BAs, MFAs, PhDs, and Grub Streeters. We are empaths, spiritual healers, babysitters, scientists, psychologists, consultants, executives, investment strategists and day-traders, higher education professionals and musicians. But most of all, we are writers and we are one WritersAnonymous.

While it is true that many of us have gone on to graduate from college, this fact is merely a product of our time. All of us are fully aware that many of the great writers of the past did not graduate from college (Fitzgerald, Hemingway, Kerouac, Poe, and Whitman just to name a few) and that college is not a substitute for the kind of talent and strenuous dedication it takes to become a great writer. We are not defined by our past. Rather, these experiences are a part of who we are and a part of each writer's journey, not unlike what life in Paris was to Hemingway and being 'on the road' was to Kerouac.

Speaking of 'on the road,' you'll be interested to know that during its final revision, the manuscript of this book made the 3,000-mile trek, in Kerouacian style, from LA to Boston with stopovers in Reno, Denver, Chicago, Detroit, and New York. So it's more than fair to say that Jack would be especially proud of the writer and book that knows what it means to literally and literarily be 'on the road.'

Lime Andersen

Among many things, Lime Anderson is a writer. "Normal," plays little to no role in her life, a philosophy that keeps her sane. She joined WritersAnonymous to provide her the "oomph" and inspiration to keep practicing the art of the written word. She believes we all bring something unique to the table and our imaginations keep us young and fresh. Her parting words? "May the muses inspire you."

Otis Anderson

Otis Anderson has been found carving unsettling memoirs on the bathroom door at The Sevens. Her hobbies include studying anatomy textbooks, and listening to a variety of jazz, R&B, and soul radio programs. Her short fiction has appeared in *Microchondria: A Collection Of Forty-Two Original Short Stories*, *Rumble* magazine, and *fictiondaily.org*.

Uncommon Bostonian

Born and raised in Washington DC, Uncommon Bostonian is a writer with Asperger's Syndrome who was with the Boston Now newspaper. After the newspaper folded in April 2008, she started a blog, titled Uncommon Bostonian, while maintaining her other blog, Outside In. She named herself "Uncommon Bostonian" because she doesn't like sports, says "Harvard" instead of "Hahvahd," doesn't drink alcohol excessively into oblivion, and frequently disagrees with retired local DJ Charles Laquidara. She is a graduate of Emerson College, class of '86.

Charles Chestnut

Mr. Chestnut is a native of Los Angeles who has called Boston home since the dot-com boom, when he nearly started Facebook with friends until he realized he was a man of letters, not computer code. He holds degrees from UC Berkeley and Harvard and will soon start an MFA in Creative Writing at the University of Massachusetts, Amherst. He writes fiction primarily (short stories and a budding coming-of-age/historical novel), but also dabbles in poetry and seven-word memoirs. He likes short walks on the beach, is a junk-food vegetarian, channels Michael Jackson on the dance floor, plays guitar concerts for his apartment building's enjoyment, and rocks the karaoke mike with gusto.

Kenton Ethan Clarke

Kent ("Clarky" to his friends) says he was one of the worst rugby players in the history of the Goldsmiths College. Despite Clarky's questionable skills on the rugby pitch at Loring, he says it sure was a hell of a good time. He misses London and Lucy, Maryanne, and Thea, the artists. He often and fondly refers to the time when the girls slyly broke into his room when he wasn't there and reassembled a replica of his room, bed and all in the middle of the common area of the hall. He also misses hanging out at the Hoy with mates Iain, Ralphy, and Gisella, and at The Rosemary Branch, affectionately known as The Rosie and run by John Laws. "There," Kent says often, "we enjoyed many a pint of diesel and snakebite with fellow rugby lads, Stevey, Martin, Paul (the skipper), and Glynn, the meanest most serious looking gentleman you'll ever meet." With tweed sport coat over a gray hoodie, a newsboy resting neatly up on his head and tobacco pipe, his friends often joke with him about his contemporary but gentlemanly style. When you meet Kent, you'll have to excuse him; he is still coming to terms with his nerdiness.

J. Lindall Derne
J. L. has deep roots planted in the Greater Boston area. It is his outspoken belief that the key to writing at all is to keep the company of good writers and better bourbon. After many years of technical and scientific writing, Derne has a longing to explore the more literary hemispheres (or whatever smaller portion of neural real estate that it might occupy) of his brain. Although he continues to grapple with a 39-year bout of writer's block, his long-time affiliation with one very supportive member of WritersAnonymous keeps him dancing on the threshold of finding his literary voice.

Falcon Canthearthe Falconer
Falcon Canthearthe Falconer likes watching *Bonanza* and *Space Godzilla* on his RCA Electrotune color TV. He is good at both goal-directed conversations and small talk. And to his delight, the park ranger told him that it's okay to keep looking for Big Foot.

Grant Trenton Gardner
Grant is a poet at heart, but not necessarily by profession. He often feels like a beatnik even though his friends tell him otherwise. He also considers himself an idealist with(out) any illusions. Get the idea? Grant is an anonymous writer in some part by choice, a seven-wordsmith, a part-time statesman, humanist, and philosopher. He can usually be found at The Sevens with a copy of *Leaves of Grass* and a yellow pad of paper with every inch covered; on foot strolling about the student center, the neighborhood streets and courtyards of Northeastern's campus (a place which he describes as truly alive); in

other scholarly hangouts such as the Espresso Royale café on Gainsborough Street, Boston; at Bakey's Restaurant downtown: a living breathing *Nighthawks* (Edward Hopper) and a place where Grant and Scottie F. met for the first time; traversing Harvard Square; as well as walking the haunted halls of the Parker House and the Boston Athenaeum.

Scottie F. Gerald

Scottie F. is an incurable romantic. Few things in life seduce Scottie as much as that perfectly crafted sentence in which every word is exactly where it belongs. Scottie believes creative writing takes care of itself when craft, imagination, and life experiences cohabitate and inform one another. To her, imagination is the panacea to the human condition. She describes adults as creatures who have already made up their minds. And for that reason alone, she has no desire to grow up. While she doesn't like to play favorites, she calls New York the unofficial center of the forever-expanding universe. Scottie F. lives aimlessly in the company of espresso, books, emotions, all creatures, humor, and imagination, and always in that exact order.

Temple Goodwin

Temple Goodwin's wanderlust has brought her to nearly 50 countries, and provided countless adventures, some of which have found their way into her writing. She's part sailor, dancer, problem solver, and wants to be the lead singer in a band, even though she can't really sing. She has recently put down the novel she was working on to begin a volume of short stories whose characters kept tugging at her, asking to be heard.

E. E. Gowings

e.e. gowings fled the west for the east to discover her identity in the deep crevices of old New England cobblestones. Having tripped on the cobblestones with the wrong boots in inclement weather, she realized she had done it all wrong. By trying to flee her self-inflicted lack of "hipness," she unknowingly clung to it even harder. But through raging blizzards, no free "paaahkkking," and the general quarter-life crisis, she needed saving. When WritersAnonymous came to her rescue, she found herself in the hidden corner of a quaint section of Boston. Really, she just showed up for the famous bowls of chili at The Sevens pub but ended up being dragged into contributing stuff for a book. Whatever.

Pinckney Phillips
A compulsive reader, Pinckney came to WritersAnonymous looking for support and motivation to make the transition from reader to writer. Along the way, she was sidetracked into the world of film. In any format, though, she firmly believes that the key to happiness is a well-told story and is on a mission to find and tell as many as she can.

L. S. Russell
If she's not saving whales from being slaughtered in the China Sea, ice climbing, or jumping out of airplanes at ten thousand feet, you'll typically find her with pen in hand. And, if not writing, she'll be at WritersAnonymous hanging out at The Sevens with fellow writers. She's a scholar and a lady, not to mention probably one of the nicest people you'll ever meet. But don't mess with her because she holds several degrees in the arts, martial arts that is.

Myrtie West
Myrtie West became smitten with esoteric healing as a second grader when a man moved in next door and confessed to her that that there is more than meets the eye happening "in the human plane" of existence. When not doing deep transformational work on herself, her clients, neighbors, cat, or the unsuspecting person who just happens to sit down next to her on the subway, Myrtie can be found exploring health food stores on the hunt for new foods, herbs, wisdom, and the ever-elusive perfect salad bar. She likes to spend time with her husband flying their little airplane around New England exploring quaint, mountain towns.

Adair Willow
Adair Willow is a transplant Bostonian with a penchant for science fiction and fantasy. She first fled her cornfields of Maryland in 2002 when she was lured to the city by Emerson College, where she earned a BFA in Writing, Literature, and Publishing. Adair works office jobs to pay rent and support her addiction to writing and local bands.

M. Zd

A former financial consultant, M. Zd left her corporate job to pursue travel and aiding those in need. She is a seasoned globetrotter, an expert on Vietnam, and a promoter of volunteering opportunities via the blog SaigonOLPC. Prophetically, she authored a research paper on holding the Olympics in her hometown Sochi, Russia, 10 years before it was chosen to host the XXII Winter Olympic Games. Being too early has always been her problem. She is an above-average chess player, amateur pianist, and a book club organizer. Her articles have appeared in an NYC based Russian newspaper.

ABOUT THE ILLUSTRATORS

Darren Buchanan
Darren Buchanan is a lifelong art hobbyist from Detroit, MI. His work is divided between pictographic poetry, meticulously enshrined ephemera, and vulgar comedy. Available in both book and video formats, you can see more of his visual artworks at bloodworld.org. Mr. Buchanan has also crafted sound shapes with various musical instruments and in several ensembles including currently playing bass in Sister Spaceman.

Kathleen Whipple
Kathleen Whipple has been called irresponsible, perverse, and awkward by her peers. She got her start as an artist when she never went backpacking across Europe. Her mother always hoped she would become a cartooning bartender. Kathleen is currently working on a series of nude early 20th-century British philosophers in watercolor. She lives in Albany, NY, teaches ethics, and enjoys urban spelunking.

THE NOT-SO-ANONYMOUS

The power and meaning of only seven words is more than illustrated below. Here's a collection of seven-words selected from the not-so-anonymous among us. However, it is worth pointing out that many of the writers and poets listed here in this section were indeed anonymous at one time. And some were rarely published if at all during their lifetime, and therefore did not receive the recognition that they deserve and receive today. In fact, most of the writers listed below all began largely in the same spot: a place of anonymity and inexperience. But, every noble writer must decide to take on that long and tedious journey, and slow and difficult process, if they stand any chance of succeeding in the long run. A process, which at times, Hemingway described as "…drilling rock and then blasting it out…" Often it is said about works of art that only time will tell of its significance. In this case, for the writers included below, time has spoken well and in volumes.

While some of the seven-words have been referenced as originally written, others have been abridged without adding or changing any words, and with every intention to preserve the original thought and meaning. The original quotations listed here can be found online at www.brainyquotes.com unless otherwise noted.

Make each day both useful and pleasant.

—Louisa May Alcott[20]

I alone presented a replica of childhood.

—Neal Cassady[21]

---

[20] **Louisa May Alcott** (1832 – 1888), **Rebecca Lee Crumpler** (1831 – 1895), **Frederick Douglass** (1818 – 1895), **Harriet Tubman** (1822 – 1913), and **Sojourner Truth** (1797 – 1883) all spent time in Beacon Hill. However, **Alcott** based her novel *Little Women* (1868) largely on her childhood experiences at her family's Orchard House (now Museum) at 99 Lexington Road Concord, MA. **Crumpler** was the first African-American woman to become a physician in the United States (1864). Her seven-words were taken from her book, *A Book of Medical Discourses* (1883). Douglass, Tubman, and Truth were abolitionists who spoke at The African Meeting House built in 1806 in Beacon Hill, the oldest black church edifice still standing in the United States. **Douglass** also served as an adviser to President Abraham Lincoln during the Civil War, and an unlikely friendship was forged over several visits to the White House during this time. **Tubman**, born Araminta Ross, was an African-American abolitionist and humanitarian. When the American Civil War began, Tubman worked for the Union Army, first as a cook and nurse, and then as an armed scout and spy.

[21] **Neal Cassady** (1926 – 1968), **Alan Ginsberg** (1926 – 1997), and **Jack Kerouac** (1922 – 1969) met in New York and became fast friends. And, together they became writers, leaders of a movement and legends, influencing American literature and generations to come. All were major figures of the Beat Generation of the 1950s. **Jack Kerouac** was considered the father of the Beat movement, a term that he disliked. His much acclaimed book *On the Road* (1957) was drafted only in three weeks on one, long scroll of paper, endlessly improvised to a beat like jazz musicians. It is rumored that **Neal Cassady** was the inspiration for Dean Moriarty. Who is Warby Parker? Warby Parker is the name of a funky retro web based eyeglass company that *GQ* and others have been raving about. It turns out that they got the name from Jack Kerouac. Their website explains: "Why did we name our company Warby Parker? We've always been inspired by the master wordsmith and pop culture icon, Mr. Jack Kerouac. Kerouac inspired a generation to take a road less traveled and to see the world through a different lens. Two of his earliest characters, recently uncovered in his personal journals, bore the names Zagg Parker and Warby Pepper." Later in the 1960s, **Bob Dylan** (1941 –) an American singer-songwriter, musician, poet, and painter led the next generation in freedom of creative expression. Dylan published the first part of his autobiography, *Chronicles: Volume One* (2004), which was nominated for a National Book Award for non-fiction. The Pulitzer Prize jury awarded him a special citation in 2008 for "his profound impact on popular music and American culture, marked by lyrical compositions of extraordinary poetic power."

Reared by a kind aunt in Pennsylvania.
I sought every opportunity to relieve sufferings.
I devoted my time, best I could.

—Rebecca Lee Crumpler[20]

Listen; a universe next door: let's go.
Once we believe, we can risk curiosity.

—E. E. Cummings[22]

---

[22] The poets include **E. E. Cummings** (1894 – 1962), **Robert Lowell** (1917 – 1977), **Frank O'Hara** (1926 – 1966), **Sylvia Plath** (1932 – 1963), **Alan Seeger** (1888 – 1916), **Dylan Thomas** (1914 – 1953), and **Frank Lloyd Wright** (1867 – 1959). You may ask why Wright is listed here among the poets when he was an architect? Well, Wright considered himself a poet, first and foremost. A poet of a different kind, but a poet just the same. As an architect, Wright was a poet of designed space and of geometric angles. **Edward Estlin Cummings**, popularly known as E. E. Cummings or often written as e.e. cummings (in the style of many of his poems) was an American poet, painter, essayist, author, and playwright. His body of work consists of nearly 2,900 poems, two autobiographical novels, four plays and several essays, as well as numerous drawings and paintings. He is remembered as a preeminent voice of 20th century poetry. **Robert Traill Spence Lowell IV** was an American poet considered to be the founder of the confessional poetry movement. Lowell was born to a Boston Brahmin family that included poets Amy Lowell and James Russell Lowell. He was appointed the sixth Poet Laureate Consultant to the Library of Congress where he served from 1947 until 1948. He won the Pulitzer Prize in 1947 and 1974, and the National Book Award in 1960. **Francis Russell O'Hara** was an American writer, poet and art critic. He was a member of the New York School of poetry. In college, O'Hara majored in music but his attendance was irregular and his interests disparate. He wrote impulsively in his spare time. During college, O'Hara met John Ashbery and began publishing poems in the Harvard Advocate. Despite his love of music, O'Hara changed his major and graduated from Harvard in 1950 with a degree in English. After receiving his M.A. in English literature from Michigan in 1951, he moved to New York City and began teaching at The New School. **Sylvia Plath** was an American poet, novelist and short story writer. She was born in Massachusetts and attended college in Northampton, MA before receiving acclaim as a professional poet and writer. She married fellow poet Ted Hughes in 1956. Following a long struggle with depression, Plath committed suicide in 1963. Plath is credited with advancing the genre of confessional poetry and is best known for her two collections *The Colossus and Other Poems* and *Ariel*. In 1982, she became the first poet to win a Pulitzer Prize posthumously for *The Collected Poems*. She also wrote *The Bell Jar*, a semi-autobiographical novel published shortly before her death. **Alan Seeger** was an American poet who fought and died in World War I serving in the French Foreign Legion. He was killed in action at Belloy-en-Santerre on July 4, 1916. He is perhaps best known for his poem *I Have a Rendezvous with Death*, which was published posthumously (1917). T. S. Eliot, Seeger's classmate at Harvard said that, "Seeger was serious about his work and spent pains over it." **Dylan Marlais Thomas** was a Welsh poet and writer who wrote exclusively in

Ask to be free. Butterflies are free.

—Charles Dickens[23]

I dwell in possibility... who are you?

—Emily Dickinson[24]

English. In addition to poetry, he wrote short stories and scripts for film and radio, which he often performed himself. His public readings, particularly in America, won him great acclaim. His sonorous voice with a subtle Welsh lilt became almost as famous as his works. His best-known works include the "play for voices" *Under Milk Wood* (1953) and the celebrated villanelle for his dying father *Do not go gentle into that good night* (1951). He was a frequent patron of The White Horse Tavern that also included other notable patrons like Jack Kerouac who got bounced out of the establishment on more than one occasion. Someone scrawled on the bathroom wall: "JACK GO HOME!" **Frank Lloyd Wright**, born Frank Lincoln Wright, was an American architect, interior designer, writer, educator, and yes, poet who designed more than 1,000 projects that resulted in more than 500 completed works. Wright promoted organic architecture (exemplified by Fallingwater). His work includes original and innovative examples of many different building types including offices, churches, schools, skyscrapers, hotels, and museums. Wright also often designed many of the interior elements of his buildings such as the furniture and stained glass. Wright authored 20 books and many articles, and was a popular lecturer in the United States and in Europe. His colorful personal life often made headlines. Already well-known during his lifetime, Wright was recognized in 1991 by the American Institute of Architects as "the greatest American architect of all time."

[23] **Charles Dickens** (1812 – 1870) arrived in Boston on November 19, 1867. It was his second visit to America and to Boston. Dickens stayed at the Parker House. Dickens is believed to have given his first informal reading of *A Christmas Carol* to a small group called "The Saturday Club," of which **Ralph Waldo Emerson** (1803 – 1882) and **Nathaniel Hawthorne** (1804 – 1864) were members. Emerson was an American essayist, lecturer, poet, and champion of individualism who led the Transcendentalist movement of the mid-19th century. Emerson is also considered to be one of the greatest American thinkers. Emerson's House and Museum is located at 28 Cambridge Turnpike, Concord, MA. Hawthorne, a novelist and short story writer was born in Salem, MA. His ancestors include John Hathorne, a judge during the Salem Witch Trials. Nathaniel later added a "w" to make his name "Hawthorne." Hawthorne anonymously published his first work, a novel titled *Fanshawe* in 1828.

[24] **Emily Dickinson** (1830 – 1886) dwelled for much of her life at 280 Main Street, Amherst, MA (now Emily Dickinson House and Museum). Not far up the street is Robert Frost Library. **Robert Frost** (1874 – 1963) was an American poet. The four seven-words incorporated in this section were taken from the poem *The Road Not Taken* (1915). Many of Robert Frost's original works can be found in Special Collections at Jones Library at Amherst College, Amherst, MA. **John F. Kennedy** (1911 – 1963) considered Frost his favorite poet and invited Frost to speak at his Presidential inaugural address. Notice that the poet and the president died in the same year. President Kennedy visited Amherst College in October 1963, a month

I prefer to be true to myself.

—Frederick Douglass[20]

There is nothing so stable as change.

—Bob Dylan[21]

Always do what you are afraid to.

—Ralph Waldo Emerson[23]

Either you think, or others have to.

—F. Scott Fitzgerald[25]

---

before he was assassinated to participate in a groundbreaking ceremony for the Robert Frost Library. Today, you can go hear President Kennedy speak in his own words (for real) at The John F. Kennedy Presidential Library and Museum located at Columbia Point in Boston, MA. The seven-words by Kennedy were abridged from a commencement address at American University in Washington, DC on June 10, 1963.

[25] **Francis Scott Key Fitzgerald** (1896 – 1940), **Ernest Hemingway** (1899 – 1961), **James Joyce** (1882 – 1941), and **Gertrude Stein** (1874 – 1946) were all writers living in Paris during the 1920s. The novelist, **F. Scott Fitzgerald** is considered by many to have written the greatest American novel. But this wasn't always the case. *The Great Gatsby* went through two printings and years later, some of these copies were still unsold. When Fitzgerald died in 1940, his obituary in The New York Times mentioned Gatsby as evidence for the great potential that Fitzgerald never reached. Yet today, in perfect condition with dust jacket, a first edition of *The Great Gatsby* (1925) could fetch as much as $250,000. Quick check your bookshelves. **Ernest Hemingway** was an American author and journalist. His distinctive writing style is characterized by economy and understatement. *The Old Man and The Sea* was first published in 1952. In a letter to his publisher in 1951, Hemingway said, "This is the prose that I have been working for all my life that should read easily and simply and seem short and yet have all the dimensions of the visible world... It is as good prose as I can write..." *The Old Man and The Sea* was awarded the Pulitzer Prize in 1953. It is believed that his little book is the reason that Hemingway was awarded the Nobel Prize for Literature in 1954. In his autobiography *A Moveable Feast* (1964), he captures what it was to live and write in Paris during the 1920s, and writes about his friendship with Fitzgerald, Joyce, and Stein. In addition to *A Moveable Feast*, two other novels *Islands In The Stream* (1970) and his unfinished manuscript *The Garden of Eden* (1986) were published posthumously. Hemingway suffered from severe mental illness in his latter years. He committed suicide on July 2, 1961. **James Joyce**, the Irish novelist and poet was considered one of the most influential writers in the modernist avant-garde of the early 20th century. Joyce is best known for *Ulysses* (1922), a landmark novel which perfected his stream-of-consciousness technique and combined nearly every literary device available in a modern re-telling of *The Odyssey*. **Gertrude Stein** was an American writer, poet, and art collector who spent most of

TWO roads diverged in a yellow wood.
And sorry I could not travel both.
I took the one less traveled by.
And that has made all the difference.

—Robert Frost[24]

Fortunately art is a community effort endeavoring.

—Alan Ginsberg[21]

Life is made of marble and mud.

—Nathaniel Hawthorne[23]

I learned a great deal from listening.
We are all apprentices in a craft.
Write the truest sentence that you know.
Finally I would write one true sentence.
Then I would go on from there.
There is never any end to Paris.

—Ernest Hemingway[25]

There is one day that is ours.

—O. Henry[26]

---

her life in France. Stein was a student of psychologist William James. With James's supervision, Stein studied normal motor automatism, a phenomenon hypothesized to occur in people when their attention is divided between two simultaneous intelligent activities like writing and speaking. Following her death in 1946, more than twenty thousand letters written and received by her were donated and bequeathed to the Yale Library. A selection of the letters written to Stein can be found in *Flowers of Friendship* (1953).

[26] **O. Henry** (1862 – 1910) was the pen name of William Sydney Porter. O. Henry gathered ideas by loitering in hotel lobbies and later Pete's Tavern. While serving time in prison in Texas for embezzlement in connection with his employment at a bank (which he denied), Porter wrote under various pseudonyms but became best known as "O. Henry." His most productive writing period began when he moved to New York City in 1902. There, he wrote 381 short stories. He wrote a story a week for more than a year. His wordplay and wit, characterizations, and plot twists were highly regarded by his fans even though critics often panned him.

Every calling is great when greatly pursued.

—Oliver Wendell Holmes, Sr.[27]

An inexhaustible good nature is most precious.

—Washington Irving[28]

Believe... and your belief will help create.
Human life... Deep experience is never peaceful.

—Henry James[28]

The smithy of my soul... uncreated conscience.

—James Joyce[25]

---

[27] **Oliver Wendell Holmes, Sr.** (1809 – 1894) was an American physician, professor, and author, and was regarded by his peers as one of the best writers of the 19th century. His works were often published in *The Atlantic Monthly*, a magazine that he named. **Henry David Thoreau** (1817 – 1862) is one of the greatest American authors, poets, abolitionists, naturalists, philosophers, and transcendentalists of the 19th century. Thoreau's writing influenced the political thoughts and actions of leaders such as Leo Tolstoy, Mahatma Gandhi, and Martin Luther King, Jr. Thoreau's experiences while living at Walden Pond, Concord, MA inspired his book *Walden* (1854). Holmes and Thoreau were known to meet regularly at the Parker House for convivial conversations over dinner with other members of the Saturday Club.

[28] **Washington Irving** (1783 – 1859) was an American author, essayist, biographer, and historian of the early 19th century. He was best known for his short stories "The Legend of Sleepy Hollow" and "Rip Van Winkle," both of which appear in his book *The Sketch Book of Geoffrey Crayon, Gent.* (1819). In 1809, Irving published his satirical *A History of New York* under the pseudonym *Diedrich Knickerbocker*, and since that time "Knickerbocker" is synonymous with New York City. Irving was also the inspiration for our advertisement at the beginning of this book (p.1). **Henry James** (1843 – 1916) was an American-born writer who was regarded as one of the key figures of 19th-century literary realism. His brother, the philosopher and psychologist William James, the gentleman kind enough to grace the back cover of our book from beyond the grave, and the prolific author of 143 books, is widely considered the father of American psychology. Henry James spent the last 53 years of his life in England eventually becoming a British subject in 1915, one year before his death. His method of writing from the point of view of a character within a tale allowed him to explore issues related to consciousness and perception, and his style in later works has been compared to impressionist painting. His imaginative use of point of view, interior monologue, and possibly unreliable narrators in his novels and short stories brought a new depth to narrative fiction.

WE mortals all inhabit this small planet.
We mortals all breathe the same air.
And we all cherish our children's future.

—John F. Kennedy[24]

Had nothing to offer except my confusion.
Write in recollection and amazement for yourself.

—Jack Kerouac[21]

A dream you dream is a dream.
A dream you dream together is reality.

—John Lennon[29]

---

[29] What do a Beatle and two presidents have in common? The answer is plenty. **John Lennon** (1940 – 1980), **Abraham Lincoln** (1809 – 1865), and **John F. Kennedy** (1917 – 1963) were all writers. All three sought to bring about social change. And all three were assassinated. **John Winston Ono Lennon** was an English musician and singer-songwriter who rose to worldwide fame as one of the founding members of The Beatles. With fellow Beatle Paul McCartney, he forged one of the most successful songwriting partnerships of the 20th century. Until he died, he remained an outspoken advocate for peace. As Lennon returned home on the evening of December 8, 1980, he was shot and killed outside The Dakota building located at 1 West 72nd Street in Manhattan. **John Fitzgerald Kennedy** ("Jack" to his friends) was the 35th President of the United States, serving from 1961 until his assassination in 1963. Before becoming president, he served in the U.S. House of Representatives and U.S. Senate. While serving in the Senate, he wrote a biography *Profiles in Courage* that won him a Pulitzer in 1955. He was also instrumental in the Civil Rights struggles of the 1960s. President Kennedy was shot and killed by Lee Harvey Oswald in Dallas on November 22, 1963. Kennedy was a great admirer of Abraham Lincoln because of his intellect and wit, and perhaps most of all for his humility. In fact, Kennedy's funeral procession, horse, and carriage were that of Lincoln's. It seems that he wasn't alone in his admiration of Lincoln. Walt Whitman, the Good Gray Poet himself would pen a poem after Lincoln's assassination, adding it to later editions of *Leaves of Grass* and calling out to the beloved dead President, "O Captain! My Captain!" During the Civil War, Whitman volunteered as a nurse and would sit for long stretches of time at the bedsides of the wounded and dying Union and Confederate soldiers. He spent so much time with these men, trying desperately to comfort them, that he could barely walk himself. His experiences during the war left an indelible mark on later versions of *Leaves of Grass*, turning it into the book it is today. **Abraham Lincoln** was the 16th U.S. President, serving from March 1861 until his assassination. As president, he led the country through its greatest constitutional, military and moral crisis—the American Civil War. In the end, he succeeded in preserving the Union while ending slavery and promoting economic and financial modernization. Lincoln was shot and killed on April 15, 1865 by Confederate sympathizer John Wilkes Booth at Ford's Theatre in

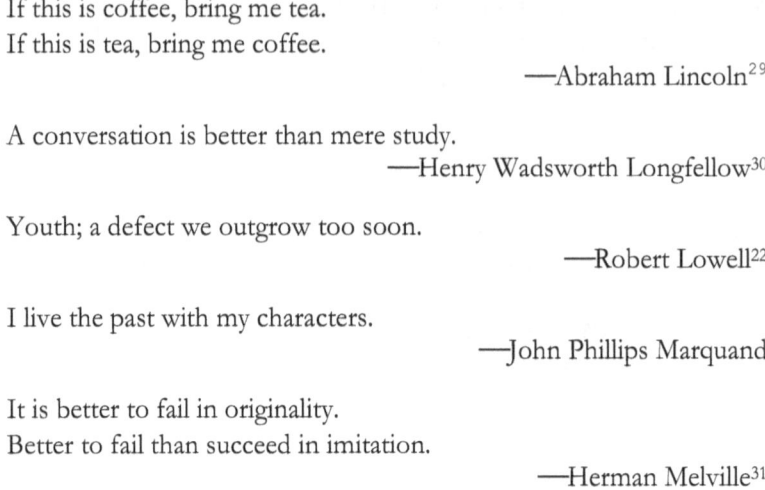

If this is coffee, bring me tea.
If this is tea, bring me coffee.

—Abraham Lincoln[29]

A conversation is better than mere study.
—Henry Wadsworth Longfellow[30]

Youth; a defect we outgrow too soon.

—Robert Lowell[22]

I live the past with my characters.

—John Phillips Marquand

It is better to fail in originality.
Better to fail than succeed in imitation.

—Herman Melville[31]

Under the illusion... had plenty of time.
Under the illusion... had time to waste.

—Joseph Mitchell

Washington, DC. Lincoln will forever be known as the man who wrote the Gettysburg Address (1863). In only 272 words and three minutes, Lincoln changed the world.

[30] **Henry Wadsworth Longfellow** (1807 – 1882) was the first American to translate **Dante Alighieri's** (1265 – 1321) *Divine Comedy* (1867, English) and was considered one of the five Fireside Poets. The group is typically thought to comprise Longfellow, William Cullen Bryant, John Greenleaf Whittier, James Russell Lowell, and Oliver Wendell Holmes, Sr., the first American poets whose popularity rivaled that of British poets. The Dante Club, another group of literary scholars dedicated to bringing Dante to light, included Longfellow, William Dean Howells, James Russell Lowell, Charles Eliot Norton, and occasional guests. The club is featured in a bestselling mystery novel *The Dante Club* by Matthew Pearl (2003). The setting is Boston in 1865 and as The Dante Club puts the finishing touches on America's first translation of *The Divine Comedy,* the group is entangled in a murder mystery even while it prepares to share Dante with the world. The Longfellow House and Museum is located at 105 Brattle Street, Cambridge, MA.

[31] Today **Herman Melville's** (1819 – 1891) *Moby Dick* (1851) is on the short list of the greatest American novels ever written. In the beginning, though, the book was received with mixed reviews. The inspiration for *Moby Dick* came from the sinking of the Nantucket whaling ship *Essex* in 1820 and from Melville's reading of Nantucket's whaling history.

I would finally renounce my delusional hypotheses.

—John Nash

There is some nicety in your words.
It's clear... I can't quite follow you.

—Flann O'Brien[32]

Pain always produces logic, which is bad.

—Frank O'Hara[22]

Everything is writable if you have guts.
I took a deep breath and listened...
Heart. I am. I am. I am.

—Sylvia Plath[22]

---

[32] Born Brian O'Nolan (1911 – 1966), most of **Flann O'Brien's** works were occasional pieces published in periodicals, which may explain why his work is not as well known as other Irish writers Joyce, Shaw, and Yeats. O'Brien was notorious for his prolific creation of pseudonyms for much of his writing. Not surprisingly, it is believed not all of his pseudonymous have been discovered. In Boston, Flann O'Brien's is also a popular pub that is largely frequented by scholars from surrounding colleges such as Northeastern, Harvard Medical School, and Mass College of Art. **James Joyce** (1882 – 1941), an Irish poet and novelist very well could have been listed here. But he was off writing *Ulysses* (1922) in Paris during the 1920s with F. Scott Fitzgerald, Ernest Hemingway, and Gertrude Stein. **George Bernard Shaw** (1856 – 1950), the Irish playwright with his distinctly trimmed beard is perhaps one of the most recognizable writers in the world. In addition to being a writer, he was also co-founder of the London School of Economics. In addition to writing music, literary criticism, and journalism, he wrote more than 60 plays. He is the only person to have been awarded both a Nobel Prize for Literature (1925) and an Oscar (1938) for the film adaptation of his play *Pygmalion*. Shaw originally refused his Nobel Prize but accepted it at his wife's request. He did however reject the monetary award, requesting it be used to translate Swedish books to English. **William Butler Yeats** (1865 – 1939) was an Irish poet and playwright, and one of the foremost figures of 20th century literature. A pillar of both the Irish and British literary establishments, he served as an Irish Senator for two terms in his later years beginning in 1922. In 1923, Yeats was awarded the Nobel Prize in Literature for what the Nobel Committee described as "inspired poetry..."

All that we seem is a dream.
Long I stood, wondering, fearing, doubting, dreaming...
The truth arises from the seemingly irrelevant.
From this purpose nothing shall turn me.

—Edgar Allan Poe

What is it… that makes them different?

—Charlie Rose[33]

Pulse nigh to pulse,... breath to breath.

—Alan Seeger[22]

A life spent making mistakes is useful.

—George Bernard Shaw[31]

Real failure does not need an excuse.

—Gertrude Stein[25]

Somebody's boring me, I think it's me.
My education… the liberty to read indiscriminately.

—Dylan Thomas[22]

Simplify your life, laws will be simpler.

—Henry David Thoreau[27]

I grew up like a neglected weed.

—Harriet Tubman[20]

Religion without humanity... very poor human stuff.

—Sojourner Truth[20]

All generalizations are false, including this one.
Emotion, if it is sincere, is involuntary.

—Mark Twain

---

[33] **Charlie Rose** is a writer, journalist and talk-show host of Charlie Rose which airs nationally on the Public Broadcasting System (PBS). He is one of the leading thinkers and curators of ideas of our time. The seven-word you see here can be taken from the transcript of nearly every show.

The muses promise to assist my pen.
Star to star the mental optics rove.

—Phillis Wheatley[34]

Behold, when I give I give myself.
Respiration... inspiration, the beating of my heart.

—Walt Whitman[29]

All fine architectural values are human values.
Every great architect is a great poet.

—Frank Lloyd Wright[22]

Walk among long dappled grass,... And pluck.
Pluck till time and times are done.

—William Butler Yeats[31]

---

[34] Born in Africa and brought to America as a slave, **Phillis Wheatley** (1753 – 1784) was educated as a child by a prominent Boston family and became the first African-American poet to be published (1773). The seven-words above were taken from the poem *On Imagination* (1773).

THERE IS ONLY ONE WAY TO WRITE

There is only *one* way to write.

—Grant Trenton Gardner

Gabriel García Márquez,[35] author of *One Hundred Years of Solitude* (1967) said, "One of the most difficult things is the first paragraph. I have spent many months on a first paragraph, and once I get it, the rest just comes..." Philip Roth[36] writes only one page a day. That's about one novel a year, give or take one year or two. And often, one

---

[35] **Gabriel José de la Concordia García Márquez** (1927 –) is a Colombian novelist and short-story writer. Although he started out as a journalist, he was awarded the Nobel Prize in Literature in 1982. He is best known for his novels *One Hundred Years of Solitude* (1967) and *Love in the Time of Cholera* (1985). His literary style is considered magical realism. He uses magical elements in otherwise ordinary events.

[36] **Philip Milton Roth** (1933 –) is an American novelist. Roth attended Bucknell University, receiving a degree in English. Then he earned an M.A. in English literature in 1955 from the University of Chicago. Roth is one of the most celebrated authors of his generation. He first received positive attention for his novella *Goodbye, Columbus* in 1959, a humorous portrait of Jewish-American life. It earned him a National Book Award in 1960. Since then he also received a Pulitzer Prize for his novel, *American Pastoral* in 1997. In addition to two National Book Critics Circle awards, Roth was also awarded the United Kingdom's WH Smith Literary Award twice for the best book of the year. In 2007, he was awarded the PEN/Faulkner award for *Everyman*, making him the award's only three-time winner.

main recurring character, Nathan Zuckerman makes his way into many of his novels. Hemingway would start a new story by writing one true sentence—the truest sentence he knew. He said, "It was easy then because there was always one true sentence that I knew or had seen or had heard someone say." Chekhov[37] said, "One has to write what one sees, what one feels, truthfully, sincerely." Whitman poured his passion into one book *Leaves of Grass*, which would end up representing his life's work and greatest achievement. Emily Dickinson wrote entire poems in one sentence. For example:

The Grass so little has to do,
A Sphere of simple Green –
With only Butterflies to brood,
And Bees to entertain –

And stir all day to pretty Tunes
The Breezes fetch along,
And hold the Sunshine in its lap
And bow to everything,

And thread the Dews, all night, like Pearls,
And make itself so fine
A Duchess were too common
For such a noticing,

And even when it dies
to pass In Odors so divine –
Like Lowly spices, lain to sleep –
Or Spikenards, perishing –

And then, in Sovereign Barns to dwell,
And dream the Days away,
The Grass so little has to do,
I wish I were a Hay –
(*The Grass*)

One of the most striking things about Dickinson's poetry is how incredibly individualistic it is. As a severely private person, she never

---

[37] **Anton Pavlovich Chekhov** (1860 – 1904) was a Russian physician, considered by many to be among the greatest writers of the modern short story. He is also known for breaking tradition with traditional storytelling practices and influencing the genre a great deal. He died at the age of 44 of tuberculosis. Chekhov's work has influenced James Joyce, Virginia Woolf, Katherine Mansfield, and countless others. Raymond Carver, who wrote *Errand*, a short story about Chekhov's death believed Chekhov was the greatest of all short-story writers.

wrote to please anyone but herself. This allowed her to be completely free and uninhibited in her writing and in her artistic expressions. There is no doubt that that led her to experiment more freely with the rules, verse form, rhyme, syntax as well as punctuation, allowing her to bend and mold the language for her purpose and desire, and in a unique and stylistic way that only few poets have been able to accomplish.

Today entire books are written in one sentence or paragraph.

At the 2011 Boston Book Festival, Michael Ondaatje,[38] the Booker Prize-winning writer and author of *The English Patient*, which also won the Academy Award for Best Picture said that when he begins writing a story, including a novel, he begins with just one simple idea like a simple conversation between a patient and a nurse, as with *The English Patient*. That is all. He never thinks about the plots or themes of his stories. They just come through his writing. And, he added that he writes his stories as a sort of patchwork tapestry. Sometimes he needs to go back to fill in the details. In the end though, it all comes together. Further, fiction for Ondaatje is based in reality but not constrained by it. That's because fiction cannot exist in a vacuum.

In his latest work, *The Cat's Table* (2011), Ondaatje included very little dialog. It is heavy in narrative, telling the reader most everything. Something that an instructor of a workshop strictly instructs writers not to do. Yet, in this 'one' example, the narrative is done with great success and style.

So, as you can see from these examples, there is only one way to write.

---

[38] **Philip Michael Ondaatje** (1943 –), a Sri Lankan-born Canadian novelist and poet, is perhaps best known for his 1992 novel *The English Patient*, which also won 9 Academy-Awards including Best Picture. He moved to England in 1954 where he later attended Dulwich College. He then relocated to Canada in 1962, and became a Canadian citizen. Before receiving his B.A. from the University of Toronto and his M.A. from Queen's University in Ontario, he studied at Bishop's University in Quebec. In 1970, he settled in Toronto and from 1971 to 1990, taught English literature at York University and Glendon College. Ondaatje's work includes fiction, autobiography, poetry, and film. He has published thirteen books of poetry, and won the Governor General's Award for *The Collected Works of Billy the Kid* (1970) and *There's a Trick With a Knife I'm Learning to Do: Poems 1973-1978* (1979).

ART & OPPOSITION

The greatest art ever made is often made in great opposition.

That's because art is passion. It makes one feel something—good, bad, even uncomfortable at times. *In The Seagull* (1896), Chekhov wrote, "It's not a matter of old or new forms; a person writes without thinking about any forms, he writes because it flows freely from his soul."

Art provokes—challenging the passive observer not only to feel but also to think and often to think differently about a given subject. More often than not, great art is an unintentional slap to the face and to the consciousness because it startles the detached observer into a response, a new experience, and perhaps a different way of seeing the world. In light of this, art will always have its critics. Yet, the artist must be willing to be as true to his vision as he can be. The opposition just comes with the territory when striving to create something new.

Simply creating opposition for the sake of opposition should never be the main objective. Art should be. Hemingway once wrote in *Death in the Afternoon* (1932) that "The individual, the great artist... goes beyond what has been done or known and makes something of his own." This desire of staying true to one's vision is what creates the spark of something truly original.

And, this is why consensus of "like" is art's greatest enemy. If the artist is after something that everyone agrees with or is pleased by, she will most likely create something watered down and not capable of great feeling, creativity or even depth. Needless to say, if the artist is after what the many will approve of, they are ensuring that no one will truly love it. And, how could they? The work is not really saying anything. And therefore, it is incapable of teaching us anything.

Chekhov violated the perceived rules of the time with regard to literature frequently and seemed to take great joy in doing so. Tolstoy said "as an artist... Chekhov has his own manner, like the Impressionists. You see a man daubing on whatever paint happens to be near at hand, apparently without selection, and it seems as though these paints bear no relation to one another. But if you step back a certain distance and look again, you will get a complete, over-all impression." Tolstoy understood that Chekhov avoided the conventional rules of storytelling consciously to recreate life as it truly is. Hemingway believed "All good books are alike in that they are truer than if they had really happened and after you are finished reading one you will feel that all that happened to you and afterwards it all belongs to you; the good and the bad, the ecstasy, the remorse, and sorrow, the people and the places and how the weather was… " (*Old Newsman Writes: A Letter from Cuba* in *Esquire*, December, 1934)

But from the same Cuba dispatch (1934), he also wrote, "The hardest thing to do is to write straight honest prose on human beings."

However, in striving to be as honest and objective as possible, Hemingway created something new, a new style of American literature. A new style of simple terse sentences largely comprised of nouns and verbs, relying heavily on rhythm and repetition. Through such understatement, the resulting effect was an unemotional and concentrated prose, capable of conveying a great deal of subtext and undertones.

Difficult as it is, we strive to write clear honest prose that sounds as if it were spoken in the real world but without all of the nonsense, stammering, meaningless words, and digressions that everyday conversation consists of. "There are some things, which cannot be learned quickly, and time, which is all we have, must be paid heavily for their acquiring. They are the very simplest things…" (Hemingway, *Death in the Afternoon*, 1932) In other words, the seemingly authentic prose is really an illusion, painstaking crafted by the writer to sound natural but for the purpose of clarity. What is important is compactness, deliberateness, flow, and the sound of prose to mimic real speech as it's being read off the page, and not grammatical correctness. Chekhov said, "Good writing should be grasped by the mind at once—in a second." And, "When a person doesn't understand something, he feels internal discord..." (Letter to A.S. Suvorin, May 15, 1889)

Writing prose is challenging because life does not happen in neat and complete sentences. Especially when we are striving to depict life and that must include prose with all of its short imperfect sounds and patterns. The necessity of a more compact and deliberate delivery of prose outweighs grammar and the importance for an actual record of what was said, as long as there is internal consistency and the reader can "read easily and simply and yet have all the dimensions of the visible world?" (Hemingway, Letter to his editor, 1951)

In addition, Chekhov said:

> Human nature is imperfect, so it would be odd to perceive none but the righteous. Literature is accepted as an art because it depicts life as it actually is. Its aim is the truth, unconditional and honest. Limiting its functions... would be as deadly for art as requiring Levitan to draw a tree without any dirty bark or yellowed leaves. The writer... must do battle with his squeamishness and sully his imagination with the grime of life.
>
> To a chemist there is nothing impure on earth. The writer should be just as objective as the chemist; he should liberate himself from everyday subjectivity... (Letter to Maria Kiselyova, January 14, 1887)

As writers, after clarity and authenticity, perhaps our highest ideal is then objectivity.

> In my opinion it is not the writer's job to solve such problems as God, pessimism, etc; his job is merely to record who, under what conditions, said or thought what about God or pessimism. The artist is not meant to be a judge of his characters and what they say; his only job is to be an impartial witness. Drawing conclusions is up to the jury, that is, the readers. My only job is... to know how to distinguish important testimony from unimportant, to place my characters in the proper light and speak their language. (Chekhov, Letter to Alexei Suvorin, May 30, 1888)

With regard to subject matter, anything can be interesting. Just as "Any calling is great when greatly pursued." (Holmes) And, "Everything is writable if you have guts." (Plath) The writers of WritersAnonymous believe this to be true. Whitman perhaps said it better than anyone.

All truths wait in all things,
They neither hasten their own delivery nor resist it,...
The insignificant is as big... as any...
(*Leaves of Grass*)

Several writers of WritersAnonymous have never been more impressed than with the use of such simplistic subject matter as in Katherine Mansfield's[39] *The Fly* (1922). Just look at how she turns a simple fly into something powerful.

> The boss took his hands from his face; he was puzzled. Something seemed to be wrong with him. He wasn't feeling as he wanted to feel...
>
> At that moment the boss noticed that a fly had fallen into his broad inkpot, and was trying feebly but desperately to clamber out again... But the sides of the inkpot were wet and slippery; it fell back again and began to swim. The boss took up a pen, picked the fly out of the ink, and shook it on to a piece of blotting-paper. For a fraction of a second it lay still on the dark patch that oozed round it. Then the front legs waved, took hold, and, pulling its small, sodden body up, it began the immense task of cleaning the ink from its wings. Over and under, over and under, went a leg along a wing, as the stone goes over and under the scythe. Then there was a pause, while the fly, seeming to stand on the tips of its toes, tried to expand first one wing and then the other. It succeeded at last, and, sitting down, it began, like a minute cat, to clean its face. Now one could imagine that the little front legs rubbed against each other lightly, joyfully. The horrible danger was over; it had escaped; it was ready for life again.
>
> But just then the boss had an idea. He plunged his pen back into the ink, leaned his thick wrist on the blotting-paper, and as the fly tried its wings down came a great heavy blot. What would it make of that? What indeed! The little beggar seemed absolutely cowed, stunned, and afraid to move because of what would happen next. But then, as if painfully, it

---

[39] **Kathleen Mansfield Beauchamp Murry** (1888 – 1923) was a writer of short fiction. She was born and raised in New Zealand and wrote under the pen name of Katherine Mansfield. She landed in Great Britain in 1908 where she met other Modernists, D. H. Lawrence and Virginia Woolf. The three writers became close friends. Among her most well-known stories are *The Garden Party* (1922), *The Daughters of the Late Colonel* (1921), and *The Fly* (1922). Mansfield is considered one of the best short story writers of her time. Mansfield was also ahead of her time in her appreciation of Chekhov. Mansfield died of tuberculosis in France at the age of 34.

dragged itself forward. The front legs waved, caught hold, and, more slowly this time, the task began from the beginning.

He's a plucky little devil, thought the boss, and he felt a real admiration for the fly's courage. That was the way to tackle things; that was the right spirit. Never say die; it was only a question of...But the fly had again finished its laborious task, and the boss had just time to refill his pen, to shake fair and square on the new-cleaned body yet another dark drop. What about it this time? A painful moment of suspense followed. But behold, the front legs were again waving; the boss felt a rush of relief. He leaned over the fly and said to it tenderly, "You artful little b..." And he actually had the brilliant notion of breathing on it to help the drying process. All the same, there was something timid and weak about its efforts now, and the boss decided that this time should be the last, as he dipped the pen deep into the inkpot.

It was. The last blot fell on the soaked blotting-paper, and the draggled fly lay in it and did not stir. The back legs were stuck to the body; the front legs were not to be seen.

"Come on," said the boss. "Look sharp!" And he stirred it with his pen—in vain. Nothing happened or was likely to happen. The fly was dead.

The boss lifted the corpse on the end of the paper-knife and flung it into the waste-paper basket. But such a grinding feeling of wretchedness seized him that he felt positively frightened. He started forward and pressed the bell for Macey.

"Bring me some fresh blotting-paper," he said sternly, "and look sharp about it." And while the old dog padded away he fell to wondering what it was he had been thinking about before. What was it? It was... He took out his handkerchief and passed it inside his collar. For the life of him he could not remember.

So with your art be bold. Take chances, even if some will surely dislike the end result. Herman Melville said, "It's better to fail in originality than to succeed in imitation." And, remember what Chekhov said. "One must be a god to be able to tell successes from failures without making a mistake." If every writer told the same stories in similar styles, the world would be a very gray and sterile place. It is true that we can all be drawn to art (a book, film, seven-word or short story) because we simply identify with the experience and are comforted by it. But, as an observer, reader or an artist, if all we ever did was to surround ourselves with art that makes us feel comfortable, then we ensure that we will never develop or realize our full potential as enlightened human beings and creative writers.

Even when going out on their own to create something bold, brave, and noble, artists cannot allow themselves to become delusional. Artists must stay grounded and humble. They must be able to distinguish between modest and great strides in their craft and recognize some need for objectivity. They must be somewhat aware of the potential impact of their work on others. Therefore, all artists need to balance what the heart is telling them with the desired effects of the art on the observer and gauge how subtle or powerful they want to be in conveying their message.

Writers should also be mindful that opposition can come from within. At the 2011 Toronto International Film Festival, Francis Ford Coppola[40] offered some advice to young writers (NPR). He said that if you write about two thousand words every day, you should become a better writer. He also believes that as a young writer, you should not look at your work soon after you've just written it because there is a hormone in every writer that makes them dislike everything they've just written. His advice is to put it away and to walk away for a while. Needless to say, give it time.

Further, writers need to be aware of external influences. This goes for editors and for technology too. Senior editor, Roger Angell at *The*

---

[40] **Francis Ford Coppola** (1939 –) is an American film director, producer, and screenwriter. He is widely acclaimed as one of Hollywood's most influential directors. He is considered part of a group known as the New Hollywood (George Lucas, Martin Scorsese, Robert Altman, Woody Allen among others) that emerged in the early 1970s with unconventional ideas about filmmaking. He co-authored the script for *Patton*, winning the Academy Award in 1970. His popularity grew immensely after he directed *The Godfather* in 1972. The film earned widespread praise from critics and changed movie-making forever. It went on to win three Academy Awards, including his second for Best Adapted Screenplay. Also under his direction, *The Godfather Part II* became the first sequel to win the Academy Award for Best Picture. Beyond the *Godfather* trilogy, he is perhaps best known for directing *Apocalypse Now*, acclaimed for its vivid depiction of the Vietnam War.

*New Yor*ker (2009) wrote, "Updike[41] was probably the very first *New Yorker* writer to shift over to a computer, back in the early eighties. "I don't know how this will change my writing," he wrote to me in advance, "but it will." He was right, of course: the flavor was mysteriously different, the same wine but of another year." Interestingly enough, Woody Allen[42] still uses the same tank of a typewriter that he started writing on. That's right, it is the only typewriter he's ever used. For 50 years, he has used an Olympia portable SM-3 that he bought for 40 dollars. And, Giles Harvey wrote a fascinating piece in *The New York Review of Books* called *The Two Raymond Carvers* (2010), which highlights Carver's successful partnership and falling out with longtime editor Gordon Lish and how his work changed after Lish.

To take a look inside the creative process, *The Atlantic Monthly* (2011) did a series of interviews with several notable creatives "On Art, Creative Thinking and Genius" called "Project: First Draft." It

---

[41] **John Hoyer Updike** (1932 – 2009) was an American novelist, poet, short story writer, and art and literary critic. He graduated from high school as co-valedictorian and class president in 1950. He then attended Harvard after receiving a full scholarship. He became widely known as an extremely talented and prolific contributor to the *Harvard Lampoon*, of which he served as president before graduating in 1954 with a degree in English. After graduation, he become a graphic artist and attended The Ruskin School of Drawing and Fine Art at the University of Oxford. Updike's most famous work is his *Rabbit* novel series (*Rabbit, Run*; *Rabbit Redux*; *Rabbit Is Rich*; *Rabbit At Rest*; and the novella *Rabbit Remembered*), which chronicles Rabbit's life over the course of several decades. *Rabbit Is Rich* (1981) and *Rabbit At Rest* (1990) received the Pulitzer Prize. Updike is one of only three writers (including Booth Tarkington and William Faulkner) to win the Pulitzer Prize for Fiction more than once. He published more than twenty novels and more than a dozen short story collections. He also wrote poetry, art criticism, literary criticism as well as children's books. Hundreds of his stories, reviews, and poems appeared in *The New Yorker*, beginning in 1954. His overriding theme was small town America and the middle class. Updike is well known for his craftsmanship and prose style. He was also prolific, writing on average one book per year.

[42] **Woody Allen**, born Allan Stewart Konigsberg (1935 –), is an American screenwriter, playwright, director, actor, comedian, author, and jazz musician. Allen has 14 Best Original Screenplay nominations from the Motion Picture Academy to his credit. He has more screenwriting Academy Award nominations than any other writer.

begins, "Great art begins with an idea—sometimes a vague or even bad one. How is inspiration…[then] the sometimes messy, frequently maddening, and almost always mysterious process of creating something new… refined into the forms that delight or provoke us?" It is worth a look.

Art is always pushing the boundaries. But only if the artist is willing to strive, to push to create something of her own, and allow her own personal experiences to influence the work she creates. Art should be uncomfortable for both the artist and the observer. As artists, when we push our own boundaries of comfort and those of the observers, there is a good chance that some will be inspired by what we do. This is because our art will have shown them something original, causing them to see and think differently, and offering them a new experience. Among many things, art is supposed to get us to wonder whether we are making the most of our lives and living it in a meaningful way. But we will never reach that destination by steering the middle of the road, building a consensus, or playing it safe.

Chekhov once said, "I would like to be a free artist and nothing else…" (To Alexei Pleshcheyev, October 4, 1888) So, let us be free in our art! Let our own take on things and who we are shine through our work. There is more than enough room in this world and in this life for our own creative take and individualistic expressions of ideas.

Also known as art.

HERE'S TO THE CRAZY ONES
STEVE JOBS (1955 – 2011)

Here's to the crazy ones. The misfits. The rebels. The troublemakers. The round pegs in the square holes.

The ones who see things differently. They're not fond of rules. And they have no respect for the status quo. You can quote them, disagree with them, glorify, or vilify them.

About the only thing you can't do is ignore them. Because they change things. They push the human race forward.

While some see them as the crazy ones, we see genius. Because the people who are crazy enough to think they can change the world, are the ones who do. (Think Different Ad Campaign, Apple Inc. 1997)

Among the crazy ones, J. K. Rowling stepped out on her own after a divorce and trusted her intuition in trying her hand at writing *Harry Potter* (1997). In the 1920s, Hemingway followed his passion (p.150), listening to his intuition, and therefore learning a great deal on writing from well-known impressionists' paintings that hung on the walls of the museums of Paris he visited nearly everyday on his way to Gertrude Stein's place. Like Hemingway then, we can all learn a great deal from another creative visionary, in the way he lived his creative life and from his words on the importance of following your own heart.

...I want to tell you three stories from my life.

—Steve Jobs

The first story is about connecting the dots.

...It wasn't all romantic. ...[But after dropping out of Reed College] much of what I stumbled into by following my curiosity and intuition turned out to be priceless later on...

Of course it was impossible to connect the dots looking forward when I was in college. But it was very, very clear looking backwards ten years later.

Again, you can't connect the dots looking forward; you can only connect them looking backwards. So you have to trust that the dots will somehow connect in your future. You have to trust in something—your gut, destiny, life, karma, whatever. Because believing that the dots will connect down the road, will give you the confidence to follow your heart, even when it leads you off of the well worn path. And that will make all the difference.

My second story is about love and loss.

I was lucky—I found what I loved to do early in life. Woz and I started Apple in my parents garage when I was 20. We worked hard, and in 10 years [it] had grown from just the two of us in a garage into a ...company with over 4000 employees... And then I got fired. How can you get fired from a company you started? Well... [I did] and it was devastating.

I really didn't know what to do for a few months... I was a very public failure, and I even thought about running away from the valley. But something slowly began to dawn on me—I still loved what I did... And so I decided to start over.

I didn't see it then, but it turned out that getting fired... was the best thing that could have ever happened to me. The heaviness ...was replaced by the lightness of being a beginner again, less sure about everything. It freed me to enter one of the most creative periods of my life.

...It was awful tasting medicine, but I guess the patient needed it. Sometimes life hits you in the head with a brick. Don't lose faith. I'm convinced that the only thing that kept me going was that I loved what I did. You've got to find what you love. And that is as true for your work as it is for your lovers. Your work is going to fill a large part of your life, and the only way to be truly satisfied is to do what you believe is great work... As with all matters of the heart, you'll know when you find it. And, like any great relationship, it just gets better and better as the years roll on...

My third story is about death.

...I [once] read a quote that went something like: "If you live each day as if it was your last, someday you'll most certainly be right." It made an impression on me, and since then, for the past 33 years, I have looked in the mirror every morning and asked myself: "If today were the last day of my life, would I want to do what I am about to do today?" And whenever the answer has been "No" for too many days in a row, I know I need to change something.

Remembering that I'll be dead soon is the most important tool I've ever encountered to help me make the big choices in life. Because almost everything—all external expectations, all pride, all fear of embarrassment or failure—these things just fall away in the face of death, leaving only what is truly important. Remembering that you are going to die is the best way I know to avoid the trap of thinking you have something to lose. You are already naked. There is no reason not to follow your heart...

No one wants to die... And yet death is the destination we all share. No one has ever escaped it. And that is as it should be, because Death is very likely the single best invention of Life. It is Life's change agent. It clears out the old to make way for the new...

Your time is limited, so don't waste it living someone else's life. Don't be trapped by dogma—which is living with the results of other people's thinking. Don't let the noise of others' opinions drown out your own inner voice. And most importantly, have the courage to follow your heart and intuition. They somehow already know what you truly want to become. Everything else is secondary...

"Stay Hungry. Stay Foolish." [It was the mid-1970s and these simple words were written on the back cover of the final issue of *The Whole Earth Catalog*] ...I have always wished that for myself. And now, ...I wish that for you.

Steven Paul Jobs (1955 – 2011) was an American entrepreneur, visionary, leader, artist/designer recognized as a pioneer of the personal computer (Macintosh, 1984; iMac, 1998), digital music (iPod & iTunes, 2001), and cell phone (iPhone, 2007) industries. And he did it again launching the tablet industry (iPad, 2010). He is widely known as a creative genius and leader who changed the way people all over the world use technology in their daily lives. In doing so, he has been compared to another legendary innovator and industrialist, Henry Ford, creator of the Ford Motor Company. Jobs was co-founder, chairman, and chief executive officer of Apple Inc. Jobs was also co-founder and previously served as chief executive of Pixar, the most successful animation studio in the world. On October 5, 2011, at the age of 56, Jobs died at his home in Palo Alto, CA of complications from pancreatic cancer. "Three stories" above was abridged and taken from Jobs' commencement address at Stanford University (2005). The "Think Different" ad slogan above was created for Apple Inc. in 1997. It was used in a television commercial and several print advertisements until Apple switched to a new slogan in 2002. The words "think different" were created by **Craig Tanimoto**. It was rumored to be a play on IBM's "Think" campaign during that time. The text was written by **Rob Siltanen** and **Ken Segall**.

A NOTE TO THE READER

A message to the writer within: Every writer needs to begin somewhere. We need to start modestly and take those small but necessary steps (like reading more and challenging ourselves in what we read, carving out time to write consistently, enrolling in a class or workshop, joining a writers group, and getting constructive feedback). This takes courage. Like Hemingway, though, we start small and write the truest sentence we know and then go on from there. And, we remember that writing will never become easy. Not if we continually strive to improve.

However, this does not imply that the journey and the sacrifices made along the way will leave us unfulfilled. Whether planning a trip to the moon or writing about it, going into this sort of risky endeavor takes a degree of faith and fortitude. But when we "set sail on this new sea," we remember it will be difficult but it will also be the most rewarding experience that we will have ever embarked on.

WE choose to go to the moon…

We choose to go to the moon.

And, do this and the other things.

We do them not because they're easy.

We do them because they Are HARD.

We set sail on this new sea.

THAT Goal, will serve to organize us.

A challenge we are willing to accept.

Mallory climbed Everest because it was there.

Well, the stars are there and knowledge. (John F. Kennedy)[43]

So when you write, setting sail on this new sea, write to please yourself. And when you are pleased, what could be more satisfying? And, when you're finished, let your work stand alone and independently of others, self-contained as a work of art, allowing it to fall where it may. And, if you did your job well, listened close enough, staying true to yourself, did honest and sincere work, and in the end, pleased yourself, as Fitzgerald did with *The Great Gatsby* or Whitman with *Leaves of Grass*... still you may not receive the reverence due to you in a timely manner. But it is fair to say that you will in the end. And isn't that all that really matters?

---

[43] Abridged from the "Moon speech" given by John F. Kennedy at Rice University on Sept. 12, 1962.

HEMINGWAY ON WRITING

It was wonderful to walk down the long flights of stairs knowing that I'd had good luck working. I always worked until I had something done and I always stopped when I knew what was going to happen next. That way I could be sure of going on the next day. But sometimes when I was starting a new story and I could not get it going, I would sit in front of the fire and squeeze the peel of the little oranges into the edge of the flame and watch the sputter of blue that they made. I would stand and look out over the rooftops of Paris and think, 'do not worry… All you have to do is write one true sentence. Write the truest sentence that you know.' So finally I would write one true sentence, and then go on from there. It was easy then because there was always one true sentence that I knew or had seen or had heard someone say… Up in that room I decided that I would write one story about each thing that I knew about. I was trying to do this all the time. I was writing, and it was good and severe discipline.

It was in that room too that I learned not to think about anything that I was writing from the time I stopped writing until I started again the next day. That way my subconscious would be working on it and at the same time I would be listening to other people and noticing everything, I hoped; learning, I hoped; and I would read so that I would not think about my work and make myself impotent to do it. Going down the stairs when I had worked well, and that needed luck as well as discipline, was a wonderful feeling and I was free then to walk anywhere in Paris.

If I walked down by different streets to the Jardin du Luxembourg, in the afternoon I could walk through the gardens and then go to the Musée du Luxembourg where the great paintings were that have now mostly been transferred to the Louvre and the Jeu de Paume. I went there nearly every day for the Cézannes and to see the Manets and the Monets and the other impressionists that I had first come to know about in the art institute at Chicago.

I was learning something from the painting of Cézanne that made writing simple true sentences far from enough to make the stories have the dimensions that I was trying to put in them... '... trying to do it so it will make it without you knowing it, and so the more you read it, the more there will be.' I was learning very much from him but I was not articulate enough to explain it to anyone. ...If the light was gone in the Luxembourg I would walk up through the gardens and stop in at the studio apartment where Gertrude Stein lived at 27 Rue de Fleurus.

—A Moveable Feast

CHEKHOV ON WRITING

It is time for writers to admit that nothing in this world makes sense. Only fools and charlatans think they know and understand everything... And if an artist decides to declare that he understands nothing of what he sees—this in itself constitutes a considerable clarity in the realm of thought, and a great step forward. (Chekhov, Letter to Alexei Suvorin, May 30, 1888)

When you fashion a story you necessarily concern yourself with its limits: out of slew of main and secondary characters you choose only one—the wife or the husband—place him against the background and describe him alone and therefore also emphasize him, while you scatter the others in the background like small change, and you get something like the night sky: a single large moon and a slew of very small stars. But the moon doesn't turn out right because you can see it only when the other stars are visible too, but the stars aren't set off. So I turn out a sort of patchwork quilt rather than literature. What can I do? I simply don't know. (Chekhov, Letter to Alexei Suvorin, October 27, 1888)

FINAL WORD

To all the writers that dropped a line in this book: Thank You.

In the end, when all is said and done, while I sincerely believe this will not be the case, even if not a single one of the writers of WritersAnonymous ever achieves 'greatness' or succeeds at becoming a full-time writer, this was never the point with me. For the journey has meant everything. In essence, all of it has been an attempt to capture and experience the writer's life or at least to imagine what it would be like up close. It has never been about a means to an end but rather, it has been about a rewarding and splendid time spent together conversing with other serious but anonymous writers, and to a lesser extent about writing at 'seven at The Sevens.' The wonderful people that I've met and the grand friendships that I have made along the way, I would not trade it for anything.

—Founder of WritersAnonymous

THE SELF-PUBLISHER'S DILEMMA

As newly self-published and unknown independent authors, we are surely Davids in a world of Goliaths—artists up against the multimillion-dollar New York publishing houses.

And so, here we are standing on the precipice, awaiting either a catastrophic fall or newfound successes that we could only dream of. What is going to happen? No one knows. And so, we are left to wonder.

To contact and support WritersAnonymous.org, and to learn about book readings/signings, future publications, and opportunities for submissions, please follow us at www.SevenAtTheSevens.com and on Facebook at www.facebook.com/SevenAtTheSevens.

Highly recommended reading for every writer:

A Moveable Feast by Ernest Hemingway
Leaves of Grass by Walt Whitman
Reading Like A Writer by Francine Prose

WHAT THEY ARE SAYING

Funny, powerful and moving. —Profiled on NPR. Listen now at: http://radioboston.wbur.org/2012/07/02/sevens-short-storie

Seven At The Sevens is for building a successful and supportive literary community. —Princeton University Alumni Magazine

Here's my advice. Read this and be entertained and inspired. (That had 7 words. Exactly. Of course.) —Prof. Gregory Petsko, Cornell University

If you love writing, this book will make you feel connected with a passionate & funny group of people who share your love. The illustrations are memorable & sometimes haunting. The quotes from Hemingway & others will inspire you. Goes with Charlie Haden's American Dream.

—American novelist Barry Eisler, San Francisco

A stroll down Charles Street in Beacon Hill feels like a step back in time—the 19th century, in fact. Stop at 77 Charles St. & you'll find yourself at The Sevens Pub, a historic establishment that opened in 1933. If it happens to be a Tuesday night at 7, you'll often see a group of writers huddled in the left window of the pub, discussing everything from Walt Whitman to the origin of the universe. They are WritersAnonymous. —Boston Globe

As you savor these succinct musings, you realize you do not need a lot of words to convey something poignant and powerful. It is above all the brevity of the language that is the engine that provides the inspiration that, perhaps, will enable you to embrace the challenge with both trepidation and delight.

—Norman Goldman, Publisher/Editor, Montreal

On most good days, if we're not trying to suck the cerebral cortex out of some wannabe writer's eye sockets, at *The Rag* we like nothing more than the opportunity to vomit chunks on some new book. But this isn't the case with SEVENS AT THE SEVENS. Buy it & read it. —*The Rag*, LES, NYC

Did the Good Gray Ghost, Walt Whitman come back from the dead for a visit? Why the bleep should we care? At *The Howl*, questioning the universe & your place in it is a bi-weekly recurrence (which, by the way, happens to coincide with the distribution of our paper) & it's a good thing. As for the Seven-Words, while they are brief & distilled, they are diverse & speak volumes.

—*The Village Howl*, Greenwich Village, NYC

WARNING: This book may cause, even jolt you to write. SEVENS AT THE SEVENS is a-fun read & the Seven-Words are addicting. Read it. Get addicted. It's good for you & at this price, it's better than a new hat. Warby Parker frames & suspenders not included. —Hipster ChronicLAX, Los Angeles

It's in your best interest never to underestimate beautiful women or this beautiful book.   —Student, NYU

A concise text that provides the reader with endless opportunity in thought.
                                                      —Student, Williams College

Their art is cool & fresh like popping an infinite # of Tic Tac's.
                                                        —Student, UC Berkeley

Immeasurably great. Infinite thoughts in a limited space expand without bound.
                                                  —Student, Stanford University

Infinitely clever and packed full of wit.   —Student, Princeton University

Took this sleek book out to the old West End with friends. Kerouac wasn't there. We still took turns reading lines to discuss. What brilliant fun!
                                                  —Student, Columbia University

Due to this volume, our campus book club is now a writers group.
                                                    —Student, Dartmouth College

A seemingly limited work of art that is unlimited by its many perspectives.
                                                —Student, Northeastern University

In honor of this thoughtful anthology and its writers, we held our first ever "box night" at Grendel's Den, Harvard's quintessential cozy hangout.
                                                  —Student, Harvard University

Elvis Costello, Angelina Jolie, Jason Schwartzman & Michelle Obama were all spotted recently with a new book believed to be a copy of SEVEN AT THE SEVENS, often described as Hemingway meets Kerouac and all hell breaks loose. In less desirable circles, Hemingway meets Kerouac and a fight breaks out. The writers of WritersAnonymous.org are indeed living a satire of their own lives. However, this statement is both unsubstantiated & confusing. It's also rumored that Mick Jagger, founding member of *The Rolling Stones* & *SuperHeavy*, a newly formed super band (2011), Desmond Tutu, former South African Archbishop & human rights activist, & Hillary Clinton, the 67th & current United States Secretary of State under President Barack Obama have contributed to this book. But again, this statement cannot be confirmed because they are WritersAnonymous.
                                                    —The Onion, Chicago / NYC

The sheer creativity and diversity of thought delight the mind and senses. "Come quickly, I am tasting stars," Dom Perignon's famous words come to mind after his first sip of champagne.   —H. Laurent, Paris, France

A SPECIAL THANK YOU

WritersAnonymous.org and the fruit of its labor "Seven At The Sevens" has only flourished because of the generous and timely support of the following people, organizations, and institutions. Without their critical support, little of what you see here could have been accomplished.

Jill Astor-Brooks, New York, NY
Michael Bruce, Cambridge, MA
Jenny Chung, Singapore
Raji Edayathumangalam, Cambridge, MA
Elizabeth Erenberg, Los Angeles, CA
Jen Flynn, Boston, MA
Joel Gagne, Chicago, IL
Kelly Johnson, New Haven, CT
Michael Johnson, Seattle, WA
Nav Khangura, Provincetown, MA
Iain Lennon, London, UK
Jim Matheson, Lexington, MA
Julie Matheson, Lexington, MA
Grant Morris, Sydney, Australia
Rishi Patil, Mumbai, India
Vivek Ramachandran, Mountain View, CA
Heather Rosefsky, Boston, MA
Kalpana Sundaram, Mountain View, CA

A SPECIAL THANK YOU (contd.)

Alternative Fiction Institute, NYU, Greenwich Village, NY
Art Council, Guggenheim Group, New York, NY
Art & Community Initiative, Harvard University, Cambridge, MA
Beacon Hill Art Council, Boston, MA
Bloomberg Foundation for The Arts, New York, NY
Boston Art Commission, Boston, MA
Community Based City Art Project, Public Library, New York, NY
Institute of Art, Design & Innovation at Northeastern, Boston, MA
New York Center of Contemporary Fiction, Manhattan, NY
The World Headquarters of American Poetry, Manhattan, NY
The Chicago Art Fund, University of Chicago, Chicago, IL
Urban Art & Fiction Project, Columbia University, New York, NY

IN LOVING MEMORY

Severina & Vincent, Nonnie & Nonno, Grandma & Grandpa O., Mrs. Flynn, and Rob Harder, one of the kindest and most creative people anyone could know.